FOREVER BLUE

THE WEIGHT OF THE BADGE - BOOK TWO

KAYLEE ROSE

Red's Bookshelf Publishing

Forever Blue: The Weight of the Badge – Book Two

www.authorkayleerose.com

Publisher's Note: This is a work of fiction. Names, characters, places, and incidents are a product of the author's imagination. Locales and public names are sometimes used for atmospheric purposes. Any resemblance to actual people, living or dead, or to businesses, companies, events, institutions, or locales is completely coincidental.

Ordering Information:

Quantity sales. Special discounts are available on quantity purchases by corporations, associations, and others. For details, contact the "Special Sales Department" at the address above.

FBTWOTBBT / Kaylee Rose – 1st Ed.

He's not just a man in uniform.
He's my hero, my best friend, and the love of my life.
He's my husband.

The Weight of the Badge series is dedicated to
the men and women in the first responder family:
Thank you for protecting and caring for our communities.
Please don't forget to take care of yourselves, too.
Come home safe.

1

KELLIE

Why do love songs always sound better when you're actually in love?

It's the question still floating through my mind when returning from the grocery store with all the fixings for a special dinner. With each item I tossed into the shopping cart, I asked myself if the last week was a figment of my imagination. Did Deputy Lance Malloy, the officer who's drifted in and out of my dreams for the past six months, really reenter my life, giving me the chance to know the man behind the badge?

Who knew the day I busted down the door to my sister's run-down apartment, it would have such a profound impact on my life? Not only did my sister die from an overdose of illegal drugs forcing me to take custody of my soon to be four-year-old niece, Rory, but it was also the day I met Lance.

I only knew him as the handsome, kindhearted officer who stood guard while I cared for my neglected niece. His interaction with Rory and the comfort he provided us, along with his words of support during that tragic day, stayed with me. The images of Lance and thoughts of what could have been if we'd met at a different time kept me awake at night. For months, he'd unknowingly burrowed his way deep into my heart until he suddenly reappeared at the same bar my best friend, Gina, was having her bachelorette party.

The whole scenario could be lifted out of a fairytale. A chance meeting under the wrong circumstances, fate decides the star-crossed lovers are destined to reunite, fall in love, and live happily ever after. Okay, the happily ever after part may be far-fetched and is a long way off from where we are right now, but what else could the outcome be given all the universe has done to bring us together again?

However, not everything has been hearts and flowers. Dark clouds have followed Lance while he deals with the aftermath of his partner's suicide.

Remembering the events of the funeral and heart-wrenching End of Watch call from the dispatcher at the cemetery brings on a wave of unwanted tears. I've never heard anything so haunting as the silence that followed the dispatcher's voice while calling for Deputy Paul Lancaster. I will never forget the pained expressions on the faces of the men and women standing around the squad car as Sergeant Williams responded instead of Paul. His gravelly voice while taking Lance's best friend out of service for the last time, then the dispatcher's reminder that his family of blue, will continue to protect and watch over Paul's family almost brought me to my knees.

Lance remained quiet for most of that day. He couldn't hide the obvious distress or the sorrow in his eyes–the trembling of his body gave it away. I wanted to make everything better, bring comfort to the broken man next to me. It was my job to be his friend, someone he could lean on. But how?

Returning to my house after the funeral, my need to ease his pain overruled the rational side of my brain. We both agreed taking things slow was best, but after what should have been a simple kiss, the slow burn ramped up to a blazing fire.

Although I pictured making love with Lance for the first time to be a slow, sensual meeting of mind and body, it couldn't have been any better. We eventually felt the gentle caress of lovers discovering each other's bodies, but that first time spoke of uncontrollable lust, desire, and carnal passion. Something I've never felt with any other man. I have no regrets. It was the most perfect night of my life.

The niggling doubts I have about how quickly our relationship is evolving and, most importantly, how Rory will be affected have moved to the top of the list of things he and I need to discuss tonight.

We need to know more about each other, but isn't that what dating is? Learning the smallest details and discovering our likes and dislikes with fingers crossed that this is the person who will make you fall head over heels in love.

Okay, so I'm already up to my eyeballs in love with Lance. Now I can hardly wait to learn more about the man who holds my heart in the palm of his hands.

~

My knight in shining armor, Lancelot David Malloy, will be here for dinner in an hour. He hates his given name, preferring Lance. He'll most likely threaten me with more tickling if I call him Sir Lancelot, but I secretly love it. I think it fits him perfectly and matches his personality and behaviors to a T. Brave, noble, and honorable. All characteristics that are befitting of the man I love.

I hope Lance brings his appetite as I'm making a feast. Fresh, homemade biscuits and gravy, crispy fried chicken, and creamy mashed potatoes.

Singing and dancing around the kitchen to a song playing in my head, I place everything I need on the kitchen counter for tonight's meal. Once the biscuits are cut out and set aside to rise, I put the chicken in the buttermilk to marinate. I'll fry it up when Lance arrives to keep it hot and crispy.

For dessert, I decide to make my favorite root beer cake. A secret recipe handed down from my great-grandmother. I remember the special day when mom sat Leslie and me down at the kitchen table to share Nana's mysterious cookbook with us. She was close to eleven, and I was eight.

Leslie and I held hands, both shaking with excitement, waiting for our mom to make the big reveal.

"Now girls, this is Nana's super-secret recipe. It was handed down to me when I was about your age, and now it's time for me to share it with you. Are you ready?"

"Yes!" we both exclaimed in unison.

"Alright, but you have to promise to keep it a secret until the time comes to share the recipe with your own children."

"We promise, Mommy," Leslie answered for me like big sisters often do.

"Time to make Nana's famous root beer cake."

I remember being disappointed to learn the big secret wasn't a secret after all. It turns out the root beer cake recipe, like so many other family favorites, came from a page torn out of an old Ladies Home Journal magazine.

From that day on, Mom would let me help bake the cake before Sunday dinners. It saddens me to think Leslie won't be the one to pass the recipes onto Rory. That job will fall to me, but it's another reminder of the cruelty of drug addiction and how it rips families apart.

Baking time is interrupted by a call from Melanie. We've become close since Gina and Dirk's wedding and chatted a few times this week. I smile when I think of the happy newlyweds. They should be home from Hawaii late on

Wednesday night. We'll give them a little time together, but in a few weeks, Melanie and I plan to kidnap Gina for a girl's night and try to make it a regular thing. I don't want us to drift apart now that she's a married woman.

"Hey, Mel, what's up?"

"Not much, just wondering how it's going with you and Lance?"

"It's good." My heart melts when thinking of him. "Actually, more than good. It's great. It's been such a rough week for him, but last night and this morning couldn't have been more perfect." I zone out and lose focus thinking of Lance.

"Hello. Earth to Kellie."

"I'm sorry, what did you say?"

"I'm assuming you were thinking about Lance since you totally missed me inviting you and Rory to Aunt Rachel's for brunch next Sunday. We are having a small party to celebrate Gina and Dirk's homecoming."

Busted. "Yeah, I was thinking about Lance again." It's hard to think of anything else. "Brunch sounds great."

"Oh, and Aunt Rachel said to bring Lance along."

"Wait? How does she know about him?"

"Apparently, Gina was talking about him when she checked in with her mom a few days ago. They're both anxious to meet the mystery man you've been dreaming about."

"Oh, no, I'm not sure Lance will appreciate being on display."

"It's not like that. Gina was so busy at the reception she thinks she missed her chance to meet him. I played dumb and didn't tell her he wasn't at the wedding." Melanie knows what happened because I needed someone to confide in while Lance was so busy making the funeral plans. "Not my story to tell."

A beeping sound grabs my attention. "Shit, I gotta go. The

timer on the oven is going off. I need to get the biscuits baked before Lance gets here." I tuck the phone between my shoulder and ear, freeing my hands to place the baking sheet into the oven. "I'll talk to him about brunch and let you know. There's always a chance he may have to work. I don't know his schedule yet, but I know his hours are all over the place."

"Alright, call me when you know." She pauses. "And hey, Kel. I'm glad you and Lance met up again. I'll talk to ya later."

"Thanks, me too. Bye."

After placing the biscuits in the oven, my phone vibrates with an incoming text.

Lance: I'm so sorry, Kellie.

That's odd; maybe he's running late.

Kellie: What for?

Lance: I'm leaving, and I don't know when or if I'm coming back. Please forgive me.

Kellie: What do you mean?

I stare at the screen waiting for the three dots to appear that indicates he is replying, but nothing happens. Pressing the return call button, it goes straight to voicemail. I listen impatiently to his message then speak after the beep. "Lance, what do you mean you're leaving and not coming back? Where are you going? What's wrong? Please call me. I'm worried."

The pressure on my chest has me gasping for air. I fixate on my phone, willing it to ring. My head starts to throb as white dots float before my eyes. On the verge of passing out, I fall to my knees, dropping the phone on the tiled floor.

Through tears, I find the button to redial only to hear Lance's short voicemail greeting again. "You've reached Deputy Malloy. Please leave a message and I will return your call."

"Lance, please call me. I'm confused and worried. Don't shut me out. Tell me where you are, and I'll come to you. Just call me back when you get this message. Okay?"

Flashbacks of me desperately calling Leslie with no answer renders me unable to move. My instincts tell me I need to run after him, but where would he go?

Still sitting on the floor, I scooch back and lean against the cupboard and pray for him to respond. I wait for what feels like hours, but I know only a few minutes pass. One more call without success convinces me not to leave further messages. I look at his text again and let out an angry scream. "Pick up the fucking phone!"

Nothing in his message makes sense. The questions are flying at warp speed through my mind. Why did he end the message with the words forgive me? What would I need to forgive him for? What does he mean if he'll be back?

Tremors rack my body while I try to figure out what to do next. A terrifying thought crosses my mind. In a worst-case scenario, what if Lance decides to follow Paul's example? I'd like to think he's stronger than that, especially knowing how he felt finding Paul's body. Looking back, the signs of denial were right in front of me. Selfishly, I worried about myself and missed the emotional highs and lows that should have set off alarm bells.

My worries amplify tenfold. I have no choice but to call Jackson.

He picks up after a few rings. "Jackson, it's Kellie. I need help."

"What's wrong? Are you hurt? Is Rory okay?"

"We're fine. It's Lance. Have you talked to him today?"

"He called me this morning after leaving your place. I thought he was going back to your house for dinner." Jackson sounds understandably confused.

"He was supposed to come back for dinner but sent me a text saying he's leaving and asked me to forgive him, but I have no idea what that means. I'm scared that after everything with Paul, I'm worried he might..." I chew on my thumbnail instead of saying the words out loud.

"Slow down, Kellie. What else did his text say?"

"Just that he's sorry and has to leave and might not come back. Please find him for me."

"Okay, let's start from the top. He sent you a text. How long ago?"

"I think it was about fifteen minutes ago." I know he's trying to put the pieces together, but I can't help but think each minute we wait could put Lance in further danger.

"Alright. Did you try calling him?"

"Yes, about five times, but it goes to voicemail. I'm scared, Jackson."

"Okay, I'll go to his house. Once I find him, I'll call you."

"Thanks, but please hurry." My gut says he isn't home. I recognize the mood changes in him. I had them when dealing with Leslie's death too. He's pushing me away and I fear the worst.

"I'm walking out the door now. I'll call you back as soon as I know what's going on." I hear him blow out his own frustrations. "And Kellie. Try not to worry until we have a reason to. I'm in the truck now. I should be at his house in ten minutes. Wait for my call."

When Jackson hangs up, I pace between the front door to the kitchen and back again. Looking for anything to distract me, I return to preparing dinner. I strain the potatoes and remove the biscuits from the oven. They've overcooked, but it doesn't matter since I know they won't be eaten. Finding the potato masher, I take my worries and fears out on the starchy vegetable, turning it into a paste. Another dish ruined. I dump the white goo down the disposal, running hot water over the mess until it's gone.

I give up on the kitchen and move to Rory's room to clean and tackle the box of old clothes I still need to sort through. Right now, I'll do anything to take my mind off the minutes ticking by with no news about Lance.

~

A loud knocking from the entryway startles me. It must be Lance. Thank god! Running to the front door, I pull it open without looking.

"Lance, you scared me to death."

Only it's not Lance. Jackson is standing where Lance should be right now. He looks pale as if something terrible has happened.

"Where's Lance?"

"I don't know." He scrubs his hand over his face. "Can I come in so we can talk?"

I step aside and lead the way to the sitting area. Arms wrapped about my stomach; I brace myself for the worst.

"Kellie, please sit down so we can talk."

I do as he asks, willing him to hurry. The longer he waits, the harder it is to stay silent. Panic swells inside me, threatening to swallow me whole. "Just spit it out and fucking tell me where Lance is and if he's okay."

"I don't have much information for you. I went to Lance's house, but he wasn't there, and his truck is gone."

"Then, where is he? Why did he say he was leaving and not coming back?" I chew on the inside of my cheek, trying to stay in control of my emotions.

"I'm still working on that. I've sent messages out to the guys asking if anyone has heard from him. I'm waiting for everyone to get back to me." Jackson reaches into his pocket and looks at his phone. "Hang on."

Jackson enters the passcode to unlock the screen. He reads the message then hands me his phone.

Lance: Jackson, I can't stay right now. I need space to think without reminders of Paul everywhere. I need you to do me a favor and check on Kellie. Make sure she knows my leaving is not her fault.

2

LANCE

It's close to midnight and the roads are clear. The only noise is from the hum of my tires on the asphalt. Unfortunately, it does nothing to drown out the voices raging war inside my head. Three times I've turned my truck around, intending to return to Kellie, only to change direction and continue the drive to the one place I hope to find peace. With my parents still in Italy, their house will act as a quiet sanctuary.

The shock of Paul's suicide has worn off and the reality he is never coming back has slammed into me with a force I can no longer ignore. When reporting for my next shift, Paul won't be in the passenger seat beside me. The next time I'm on a call, he won't be there to keep me safe. Using the back of my hand, I wipe away a stream of tears that won't stop.

Replaying the last conversation I had with Jackson over and over in my mind, my grip on the steering wheel tightens, turning my knuckles white. He was right. I unintentionally used Kellie to distract me from accepting Paul's death. She was an innocent pawn in the mental game I played to avoid the reality that my partner, the man I loved like a brother, shot himself.

Taking advantage of Kellie's kindhearted nature and her need to care for others has sent me spiraling to an all-time low. Spending the night in her bed felt right at the time, but now I recognize it for what it was–a distraction. I failed Paul by not paying closer attention and getting him help before he pulled the trigger. I ignored the sense of urgency I knew was there, instead waited until my calendar was clear before setting up the necessary intervention for Paul.

Yes, I wanted to be with Kellie, but under these circumstances, I used her to forget the tragic events of the past week.

While helping Paul's parents make funeral arrangements, I had no choice but to focus on his suicide. Falling into Kellie's bed turned off the unsettling thoughts long enough to pretend I was capable of protecting and caring for another person.

The aftermath of losing my friend hurts like hell but treating Kellie so appallingly may have ruined any chance I had of pursuing a relationship with her. Twice the universe brought her into my life and twice fucked-up circumstances have prevented us from connecting. I want to believe there is something to explore between us, but unless I get my head on straight, I can't be with her. My messed-up head tells me it's best to cut the strings now before I fall deeper in love.

Escaping to my parents' house will also allow me time to think about my future in law enforcement. I planned to stay at the Springhill Sheriff's Department until retirement age. Now, I find it hard to see myself continuing in a job that will slowly eat away at my soul until there is nothing left to live for. It's part of what I think Paul was trying to tell me in his goodbye letter. Get out before I lose myself in this thankless job.

A ding from the fuel indicator tells me I'm low and has me pulling off the highway into a gas station about an hour away from my destination. Inserting my card into the reader at the pump to pay, I tense when I hear sirens in the distance. Red and blue flashing lights are visible before I see the squad car speed past. The hairs on my arms raise and a jolt of adrenaline hits my body. It only takes an audible cue and I'm instantly on alert.

Without meaning to, my eyes dance about, searching for the address of the gas station. My mind registers what I would call over the radio before waiting for my next instructions from the dispatcher.

Fuck. I huff out a breath and shake my head, frustrated. I'm not on call. Whatever is going down isn't within my jurisdiction. Just once, I want to turn off my brain and be Lance, not Lance, the cop. I know better–even if I leave law enforcement for good, my training will never leave me.

Switching on lights as I walk through my parent's house, I see pictures from my childhood on the walls—each representing another memory and milestone in my life.

It's strange to see myself develop from a child into a man in such a one-dimensional way. None of my hopes, dreams, fears, or life experiences are visible behind the glass.

Looking at my sophomore picture, I remember how that day was full of teenage angst. Even though my girlfriend just dumped me, I slapped on a fake smile for the camera and hid the evidence of the first time my heart was broken.

That emotional deception makes me think of Paul and how he hid his pain after his wife, Jane, died. There were days he would stroll into our morning meeting, full of laughter, acting like everything was normal. When in reality we spent hours on the phone the night before while he sobbed about missing his soulmate. But I wasn't fooled, just slow to react and too self-absorbed in my own life to make his a priority.

The last picture on the wall marks my final step into adulthood–graduation from the police academy. Standing beside me are both my parents. The smile I wear in this photo is authentic. Mom appears happy, but I know the truth. She hated the idea of me following in my father's footsteps and initially refused to attend the ceremony. It broke my heart, but I had to respect her decision as she did mine.

When the time came to receive my badge, I glanced into the crowd, hoping to see my father. Instead, I noticed both my parents standing in the back of the crowded room. Mom dabbed at her eyes with a handkerchief and Dad gave me a simple nod of approval.

Later, for the official pinning of my badge, Mom held my hand tight while Dad attached the brass star to my chest. At that moment, my life was perfect. I never imagined a day when I would doubt my choice to be an officer the way I do right now.

Tossing my duffle bag on the twin-sized bed in my old room, I look at the remnants of my past. Mom didn't leave my bedroom exactly as it was when I left home, but she did keep some of my childhood treasures on display.

A few trophies from high school are arranged on the high-top dresser. Pictures from Prom and an old baseball signed by some major league player I don't remember. Typical kid keepsakes that mean nothing to me anymore.

Of all the items still on display, it's the pinewood derby cars on the top shelf that still fills me with pride. Lined up in order of the year they were built, these handmade gravity-powered cars hold happy memories of days when Dad and I worked together as a team.

Dad would schedule a few personal days off to coincide with this annual tradition. We would spend hours in his workshop planning and perfecting my derby car. As a seven-year-old Tiger Cub, Dad was the one to use the power tools, but I did most of the work under his supervision.

The bright neon green car with red and blue swirls was from my first year competing. Picking it up, I inspect it closely. The axles are crooked, and the wheels are wobbly. I push the car back and forth slowly on the shelf; the evidence of my inexperience clear when the front wheels stop rolling. I return the vehicle to the front of the line and laugh.

No wonder I came in last place. This car is a piece of shit.

Back then, I thought it was unbeatable. I was confident I had just as much of a chance to win as any other scout. Placing my car at the starting line of the sloped racetrack, I cross my fingers this was my year to win, only to have my dreams crushed by the cars that were obviously built by parents.

I didn't want to be a sore loser, but how could I not feel cheated? This event was supposed to be for the scouts, not for parents to relive their childhood.

After the race, Dad tried softening the blow by taking me for a hamburger and chocolate banana milkshake at Helen's Diner. It was almost worth losing to have this special time with him since his job rarely gave us these father and son moments.

We'd talk about the ways we could improve and what changes to make for next year. Then my dad would impart a few words of wisdom too deep for me to understand as a kid in grade school, but as time passed, I began to comprehend the message.

"Even though you lost today, I'm proud of you, son. Learn from it. How can you be better? In the long run, you'll be that man who succeeds in life." He patted my shoulder. "Taking home the trophy without putting in the hard work isn't really winning. It takes effort and sacrifice to be able to call yourself a winner." He paused

before adding the last part. "Lance, find something you love, put in the effort to perfect it, make it yours. It's only then you'll find success and happiness."

Each year, I earned my Cub Scout achievement patches, allowing me to move up in the ranks. In fourth grade, Dad was able to sit back, allowing me to build the car on my own. Silver with a black stripe running from front to back. This masterpiece was my pride and joy. Lifting it out of the clear plastic display case I stored my beauty in for the last eighteen years, I study the fine details I meticulously added. The hand-painted number eight on each door, a custom snake logo on the hood, and Team Malloy in red letters proudly written in sharpie on the roof.

Start to finish, I crafted a world-class racing machine to the specifications required, finally taking home the first-place ribbon. Dad didn't change our routine that day. He still took me to Helen's for a burger and shake and gave the same speech, only instead of you lost, today he said, you won. It took a few years, but I realized win or lose, the message remains the same. Success comes from hard work and that I should never stop putting in the effort to get there.

This time, when I push my championship car across the shelf, the wheels spin fast and smooth. It moves quickly and I almost don't catch it before it crashes to the floor.

Mulling over Dad's speech again, I recognize the irony in the last part. Only now his words take on a different meaning. Find someone you love and put in the effort to make her yours. I think having Kellie in my life is where my happiness lies. I only hope, by the time I figure out how to fix myself, it isn't too late.

Toeing off my boots, I lay across the bed and stare up to the ceiling as if the answers I'm seeking will magically appear.

My life is fucked up beyond all recognition, with no easy

fix in sight. Sure, I made it worse by walking away from the woman who could be the love of my life, but Paul must take a share of the responsibility for my shitty situation too. "Fuck you, Paul! You're a selfish bastard." I'm talking to myself, but a part of me hopes he hears my words. "Because you couldn't talk to me, you ruined my chance for happiness!"

Being angry at somebody no longer there is a waste of time, but I can't help feeling pissed at him for not talking to me. His letter did nothing but leave more unanswered questions. Why didn't he trust me the way I did him? He knew all the fears and insecurities I had about my dad and let me lean on him more times than I care to admit. I showed him the weak side of me, but when he was at his weakest, he didn't do the same.

Of course, I believed Paul when he said, "I'll always have your back." He promised to be the person I could count on during the hard times, but it was all a lie. The most challenging time of my life is upon me, and he's part of the cause.

Blinking back tears, I feel the rage burn inside my chest. "I hate you, Paul!" Jolting up from the bed, I throw my prized derby car against the wall, leaving a dent in the sheetrock. The wheels fly off, scattering in different directions on the hardwood floor.

God damn it. This isn't me. Controlling my emotions, keeping a cool head, and remaining calm when others become unhinged is what I do. I pick up the pieces of the car, knowing it will take more than glue to put it back together, but it will never be the same again, just like my life.

Deep down, I know Paul would never knowingly hurt me, but I can't help thinking my heartache over Kellie is penance for not being aware of what he was going through. The universe has dangled the carrot of happiness in front of me, sending her back, only to rip her out of my arms like some cruel cosmic joke.

My feelings for Kellie are strong, but nothing like a husband losing his wife as Paul did with Jane. The more I think about it, the more I know I will eventually find a way to forgive Paul. But I'm not there yet, although I hope to find peace inside my own heart. I'm hurting, but I wish the same for Paul.

I unzip my duffle bag and remove the meager contents wanting to feel settled. Placing the extra clothes in my old dresser and bringing my toothbrush into the bathroom provides a feeling of calm, reminding me this house will always be my haven.

Before I do anything else, I need to call Jackson. If I don't tell him where I am, he'll organize a search.

Jackson has been my voice of reason during this whole ordeal and the only person I know who won't judge me. No doubt he'll kick my ass for my behavior, and I'll deserve that beating, especially for leaving him to clean up the mess I made with Kellie.

Powering up my phone, it pings from the many missed text and voice messages. Ignoring them, I pull up Jackson's number. He picks up on the first ring, obviously waiting for my call.

"What the fuck man? Where are you?" Jackson's voice is laced with anger.

"I'm at my parents' house. I'm sorry, Jackson. I didn't know what else to do."

"I get it, but you have to know your actions caused a lot of panic. It's why I didn't want you to be alone." I stay silent and listen, allowing Jackson to continue his lecture. "Hey, I'm not trying to kick you when you're down, but you scared the shit out of everyone."

"I know I fucked up, but I didn't think about it at the time. I'm sorry."

"What happened to make you run? I thought everything with Kellie was going great."

"I thought so too." I reach into my duffle bag and pull out the tan envelope with Paul's goodbye letter, patches, and photographs. "When I got home, there was a letter from Paul, and I freaked out."

"Damn, Lance. It makes sense, but you should have called me instead of running."

"You know that's easier said than done. Now that I'm thinking straight, it's what I'm doing, so give me some credit."

"Alright, I'll back off because you're right, you've called me, and I'm glad you did. What does the letter say?"

"I'll be honest, Jackson. I'm exhausted and don't want to do this right now. I just wanted to check in with you, let you know I'm okay, and ask about Kellie. Did you talk to her?"

"Yeah, I went to her house and she saw your text, but you need to talk to her yourself."

"Fuck man. I know I screwed up, but I can't call her right now. Can you let her know I'm fine and keep an eye on her? I need this time for myself. You were right. She was my distraction. I know I've hurt her, but unless I figure out how to deal with everything in my head, I'm no good for anyone."

"I get it, and yeah, I'll talk to Kellie, but you need to man up and call her soon. Can I tell her where you are?"

"Sure, you can tell her where I am and that I'm okay. I'd ask you to try and explain what's going on with me, but I don't know myself. Just tell her I'm sorry and, when I figure out what direction I'm going, I'll contact her."

"I can do that. Now, are your parents back from Italy yet?"

"Nah, they don't get home for another two weeks. It's why I figured I'd stay here."

"Dude, I don't think—"

I cut him off before he can continue. "Stop. I know you're concerned and the way I took off without a word wasn't cool. But I'm also tired of being babysat. I'm a grown man and need some space."

There's a silence between us. I know Jackson well enough to realize he is considering what to say next.

"Fine, but if I'm calling and checking on Kellie for you, you can do the same with me."

"Deal." That was easier than I thought it would be. "Hey, last thing. Can you let me know when you talk to her, please?"

"Yeah, man. I'll call you after I check in with her. She's hurting, so the sooner you call, the better."

"I know. Thanks again, Jackson. I'll call you tomorrow."

Turning the phone off, I place it on the bedside table and switch off the light. Arranging the pillow under my head, I close my eyes, praying sleep claims me quickly.

3

KELLIE

Curled up on the overstuffed chair beside the large picture window in my living room, I tuck the fuzzy pink blanket around my legs. It's the same blanket I use when reading bedtime stories to Rory. With her still at my parents', the night is quieter than I'm used to.

The text Lance sent to Jackson provides no answers about where he is or what caused him to leave town. Once I stopped trembling, I was able to convince Jackson to go home, allowing me the quiet I need to figure out what went wrong.

The crescent moon and stars shine brightly in the cloudless sky, bathing the room in dim light. This time of night would usually bring tranquility into my otherwise chaotic world, but tonight I sit in the shadows, distracted and unable to identify constellations I should know by heart from the times I sat with Rory looking through her picture book.

I seek out Polaris, the north star, once used by seafarers to navigate their way home safely. In my mind, Lance is staring up into the dark sky while trying to decide which direction to travel and if that path will lead him home.

Identifying the north star, I follow the dots to the big dipper and imagine Lance and I reconnecting.

Was it really fate? Does the universe push two people together, or is it simply a chance meeting? Are we solely responsible for our future, with destiny only a figment of our imagination?

A falling star streaks across the sky, catching my attention. Quickly, I close my eyes and make a wish.

Please let Lance be safe and if we are meant to be together, bring him back to me.

Perhaps it's childish to hope a simple dash of light possesses the magic necessary to bring me my happily ever after, but I'm willing to try anything at this point.

Recalling the events of the last week, I recognize the mistake I made, starting at Heath's bar. I allowed excitement at seeing Lance cloud my judgment. I've always been levelheaded and sensible when it comes to how I live my life. It may seem dull to anyone looking from the outside in, but it creates the stable environment Rory deserves. Being impulsive and reckless was Leslie's parenting style, not mine. I promised to do better but can't help thinking I've made another misstep while figuring out how to be a parent.

Again, I'm reminded of how challenging it must have been for my big sister, raising Rory by herself yet still craving a life away from motherhood. It doesn't excuse Leslie's drug abuse or neglect of her only child, but I allow myself to feel more compassion for the difficulties that come along with raising a child alone.

I'm ashamed for letting my emotions take over without considering the negative consequences that frequently come with new relationships. When I think of Lance, all I see is the strong, protective gentleman I've fallen in love with. The pedestal I unfairly put him on didn't leave room for anything less than perfection. I was blindsided by the intensity surrounding our meeting, not considering the adverse effects should our relationship fail to be everything I dreamed of.

I don't blame Lance. He was honest about his feelings, asking me to be his friend first and foremost, and the minute he left the door ajar, I barged through and sprinted into his arms. The right thing would have been to consider the circumstances of why he let his guard down. At the very least, recognize he was consumed by grief and using me as a distraction. I should have looked past my own wants and been the one to remain in control. My selfish behavior only made the situation worse.

Tucking my legs underneath me, I pull the blanket up under my chin and look at the moon. Last night, moonlight streamed through my bedroom window as Lance and I made love. I don't want to believe our night of passion was simply a distraction, but my head warns what my heart wants to ignore.

My temples throb with the onset of a migraine. I've already taken two headache tablets, but they don't seem to be working. I asked Jackson to call me with news, no matter the time. Until I hear Lance is safe, there's no way I will be able to sleep.

Turning my phone over to look at the screen for what seems like the hundredth time, I growl my disappointment at not getting an update.

Deciding I can't wait any longer, I impatiently begin typing out a message to Jackson when I'm interrupted by his incoming text.

Jackson: Are you awake?

Not wanting to text back and forth, I dial his number, eager for something, anything that will put my troubled mind at ease.

"Hi, Kellie."

"Have you heard anything?"

"Lance called me a little while ago. He's okay and asked me to get in touch with you."

A feeling of relief washes over me. "What else did he say? Where is he?"

"Slow down. I still don't have all the answers. We only spoke long enough for him to tell me he's doing alright and that he is staying at his parents' home."

"And you still have no idea why he left?" I seriously doubt Jackson would be satisfied with only getting a fraction of the truth.

"He received a letter in the mail from Paul. I suspect that's the biggest reason, but he isn't ready to talk about it yet."

"Oh, my God. He must be a wreck." Imagining Lance reading Paul's letter without anyone there to support him tears at my soul.

"He sounds better than I expected, but he's still struggling. He also said to tell you he's sorry."

I inhale deeply and confess my part in his leaving. "I'm the one who should be sorry. It's my fault he left. I screwed up. He trusted me to help and I let him down."

"You can't beat yourself up. You were there for him when he needed you most. Lance is a good man, strong-willed, but responsible for his own actions at the end of the day. He's weighed down with guilt over Paul's suicide and needs to figure out how he plans to move on with his life. We can't decide it for him."

I'm not convinced Jackson is right, but there's no sense arguing. "I hear what you're saying and appreciate you keeping me in the loop."

"Before I go, I have something to ask of you that won't be

easy." Jackson's pause has me on edge. "I know it's not my place, but I think it will be best if you wait for him to contact you. He needs to focus on how to move forward and deal with Paul's death without distractions. It's obvious he cares for you, but he needs this time away to heal."

Holding my breath, I hope to control the new wave of tears threatening to fall. The pounding in my head is almost unbearable. I trust Jackson and if waiting until Lance is ready to talk to me is necessary, I'll follow his lead, but it doesn't mean it hurts any less.

"Kellie, are you going to be alright?"

"I think so."

"I'll be in touch, but please don't hesitate to call me if you need anything, okay?"

"Ummm, Jackson, wait. Can you get a message to Lance for me?"

He hesitates then says, "Sure. He's supposed to call me sometime tomorrow."

"Can you tell him I'm glad he's safe?"

"I will pass that along. Now try to get some rest, and when I talk with him again, I'll call you."

"Thanks, Jackson. Good night."

With the call over, I sink into the cushions, pull the blanket over my head, and try to reconcile in my heart with the reality I won't see Lance anytime soon.

After tossing and turning all night, the drive to pick up Rory from my parents is a rough one. I make a quick stop to grab a Venti, triple shot, salted caramel, mocha. If the caffeine doesn't kick start my day, the sugar overload will whip me into shape. With any luck, the dark circles under my eyes will stay hidden from my mother under the layers of makeup I applied this morning. She knows nothing of Lance and today isn't the day to share. My plan is to bring Rory home and go about our usual routine.

I park behind Dad's old pickup truck and walk in through the open patio doors. The house is strangely quiet. Usually, I hear Rory chattering and playing loudly, but today, nothing.

"Mom? Dad? Rory?" I call out their names but still nothing. "Where are you?"

It's then I hear giggles coming from behind the couch.

"Gee, I wonder where Rory is?" More stifled laughter makes my heart sing. "Oh, well. Too bad Rory's not here. I was planning on buying some ice cream on our way home."

In a shot, Rory scrambles around the couch. "Boo!"

"Oh, you scared me!" I crouch down and open my arms to catch her in a hug. "Were you hiding from me?"

"Want strawberry ice cream, pweez?"

"You got it, kiddo. And since you said please, how about we make sundaes with lots of whipped cream?" This isn't entirely for her. I could use some ice cream therapy tonight to keep my mind off Lance.

"Yes!" She jumps around, excited, doing some crazy dance with her arms swinging back and forth. It's almost enough to make me forget about the dark spot lurking in my heart.

"Good morning." Mom appears and kisses my cheek.

"Morning. Where's Dad?" I expected to see him working in the backyard when I pulled up. My dad's pride and joy, besides Rory, is his perfectly landscaped yard. He spends hours out there gardening, then relaxing on the patio when the day gets too hot.

"He's over at the neighbors, helping them move furniture or something. You know I barely listen to him." She's teasing. They are still very much in love.

"I'm sorry, but we can't stay for dinner tonight. I have chicken in the refrigerator. I don't want it to go to waste."

The marinated chicken is the only thing that is still usable from last night's fiasco.

Mom cocks her head and shoots me a look of concern. "You look tired. Are you getting sick?"

"I'm fine, but yeah, tired. The funeral was very emotional." Shit, I didn't mean to bring up the funeral. With my luck, she'll see it as an open invitation to ask a bunch of questions.

To my surprise, she doesn't. "I understand. We can try again next Sunday."

"Sounds good. Rory, why don't you go get your bag from your room." Footsteps echo from the hall as she runs to her bedroom. It's the same one Leslie and I shared until we reached the age where we needed our own space.

"You know if you want to talk, I'm here anytime you need me." Mom brushes my hair back from my face, tucking it behind my ear like she did when I was little. Eventually, I'll share with her all that has happened, but until I know what the future holds, I need to keep it to myself.

Before I can respond, Rory runs back into the kitchen. "Gram Gram. Can I have some berries?"

"Of course, sweetie. Let me get you a container. How about the peas and carrots you picked? Do you want those too?"

"I loooove carrots." The way Rory says love makes Mom and me both laugh.

"And I loooove you." I pick her up and blow raspberries on her belly. Rory's fits of giggles have Mom and I both laughing along with her.

Glancing to Mom, we exchange a knowing look when she wipes away a stray tear. Without a doubt, she's thinking of Leslie and what could have been an amazing day with all three of her girls. I know because I'm thinking about the same thing.

~

My lack of sleep these past two nights has caught up to me. With Rory bathed and ready for bed, I pick up the book she's chosen for me to read. I doubt I'll get more than a few pages into the story tonight. She's already rubbing her eyes, fighting to stay awake.

"Scooch over so Addy K has room to lay down."

Rory lifts the covers for me to climb into her bed.

With Mr. Deputy Bear on one side, she snuggles into me and says, "I'm ready."

"Alright, let's see. What book did you choose tonight?"

"David!"

"Naughty David again? I wonder what he did this time." This series of books crack me up. The little boy misbehaves, but his parents love him even when he's up to no good. It's also about teaching him to be responsible for the things he does. I've used him as an example several times when Rory has told me it's not her fault.

Four pages into reading about David's monkeying around, I glance over to see Rory's thumb in her mouth and eyes closed in a deep sleep. I know thumb sucking is viewed as a bad habit, but we all have ways we soothe ourselves. Dr. Michaelson assures me she won't do it forever, and really, it's only when she's overly tired. Today we played for hours outside, creating masterpieces on the sidewalk with chalk before bingeing on movies and snacks. I cut off the ice cream after our second scoop.

Maybe it's down to the junk I ate today, but thinking about not being able to call Lance, has my stomach churning. Jackson sent a short text a few hours ago. He spoke with him and says he's doing okay. With not much information, I simply thanked him for the update. Hopefully, I won't have to wait too long to hear from Lance himself.

Brushing the wisps of baby hair off Rory's forehead, I whisper I love you, and walk to my own room for the night.

Reaching into the drawer of my bedside table, I take out the leather diary I started writing in soon after Leslie died.

Hi, Sis.

Sorry it's been so long since I last wrote. It seems there are never enough hours in the day to finish my to-do list. Damn, I'm beginning to sound just like Mom.

Rory is asleep already. You would be so proud of your baby girl. She is growing fast and talking so much it's hard to keep up sometimes. We read together every night and she is doing great on her sight words. Rory is a pro at flashcards with simple two and three letter words. I think those daily lessons are paying off. The days of trying to decipher what she is saying are gone.

I'm glad Mom and Dad took a lot of pictures while we were growing up. Rory and I have started making scrapbooks while we sort through them. It's important she knows her momma in heaven and I want her to have these books when she's older.

Out of the blue, she asked when your birthday is so she can buy you a red balloon. She said she wants to let it fly up to heaven so you can have a special present from her.

I almost forgot to tell you. Rory will be starting preschool in a few weeks. I was able to get her into the same school you and I attended. The Rainbow Center looks exactly like I remember with the huge castle, twisty slide, and your favorite tire swings in the playground. I know Rory is going to love it.

Guess what? Remember the officer I told you about? We ran into each other at Gina's party. I thought he was the one I was meant to be with forever. Lance is kind, protective, and seems like the perfect man to allow into our life. I've fallen in love, and I know he has feelings for me as well, but here's where things become complicated. He is dealing with his own demons and needs space to figure out how to move forward with his life. Unfortunately, I'm not sure how long that may take.

It's times like now I wish you were here to give me some sisterly advice. With the stress Lance is under, he's better off without the burden of dating a single parent. For now, I think it might be best to focus on raising Rory and put the fairytale of finding my prince charming to rest.

I better get some sleep. I'll check in with you again soon.

Rory, Mom, Dad, and I miss you every day.

Love you lots, Sis. Good Night.

4

LANCE

Waking slowly, I rub the sleep from my eyes and sit up on the edge of my mattress. Last night was the first time since Paul's death I slept without nightmares waking me in a cold sweat. It confirms my decision to leave Springhill was the correct one, even if there will be negative consequences over the way I left town.

Yesterday was spent mowing the grass, tinkering with some old model kits in dad's workshop, doing minor repairs around the house, anything to distract me from calling Kellie. I know all it will take is hearing her voice to send me into a tailspin of emotions I'm not ready to face.

Having Jackson act as a middleman makes me a coward. I should let her move on without me, but I can't find the strength to give up just yet.

I ask myself the same question which has been plaguing me over the past forty-eight hours. Is it better to ignore my feelings for Kellie to avoid heartache or follow my heart and hope for the chance to be happy? No matter how hard I try, I still don't have an answer that satisfies me.

I tell myself I will never be good enough because she

deserves a man who will put his family first. What makes me think I'll be any different than my dad? All the missed birthdays, listening to mom cry when he wasn't with us for Christmas, fears about him being hurt on the job. I don't want to think of Kellie going through that same stress.

My selfish side warns me to not let her go without a fight. Kellie is strong and can handle this lifestyle. Being a cop is honorable, and although not without obstacles, having a family is possible.

Paul and Jane seemed to make it work, and I know without cancer and its cruel intervention, they would have gone the distance. They would have made great parents. In fact, Paul and I talked about raising our kids together.

We thought Jane was pregnant once. Paul's excitement at the prospect of becoming a father lit up his face.

After another late shift, I grab my bag and call out to Paul. "I'm out. Tell Jane, I said hi. I'll see you tomorrow."

Before I could leave, Paul stops me. "Wait. Jane told me I shouldn't tell anyone yet, but you know I can't keep secrets from you. She took three tests and it looks like you're going to be an uncle."

"Congratulations! That's great news. So, one of your swimmers finally reached the finish line." They've been trying for months to get pregnant and Jane was starting to lose hope.

"Looks that way. It makes sense now. Jane has been exhausted and throwing up for the past few days." He chuckles and claps me on the shoulder. "Now it's your turn to settle down with your own family so our kids can grow up together."

"That may not be a good thing. Can you imagine our kids and the chaos they will leave in their wake?"

"Exactly my point. Paul Jr and Lance Jr will be legendary in their teens."

"But what if you have a daughter?" I can practically see the cogs turning as if it didn't occur to him that they could have a girl.

Paul's eyes narrow and nostrils flared. Without a hint of sarcasm, he growls, "She won't be leaving the house until she's thirty."

Watching him switch into protective mode has me chuckling. "Good luck with that, daddy."

We continue walking to the parking lot when I catch a few of Paul's mumbled words. "My princess will never date. No guy will ever be good enough."

He won't be the only one watching over this bundle of joy. The entire Sheriff's Department will spoil him or her with the promise to keep their child safe.

Standing between our trucks, I pull him into a hug and congratulate him again. "I'm happy for both of you."

His smile returned to a sappy grin. "Thanks, buddy. I'll see ya tomorrow." Climbing into his truck, he rolled down the window and shouted to the world, "I'm gonna be a daddy!"

Unfortunately, the symptoms Jane had were cancer related. It was the first time I felt utterly helpless. No matter how much I wanted Jane to be healthy, I was incapable of making it happen.

It's the same sense of powerlessness I feel now. A few words of advice from our academy instructor come to mind. He spoke of ways to remain calm and professional while on the job, but his message seems fitting at this moment.

"It's imperative for you to remember you have no control over what others do. It's up to each of you to keep your emotions in check, focus on changing your own behavior and reactions to the situations around you. Once you learn to accept what you can't control, you will find you have the upper hand."

Deep down, I know I couldn't stop Paul. He made his choice, and nothing I do will bring him back. Wallowing in grief is a waste of energy. It would be crazy to think my pain will disappear completely. I will continue to miss Paul and Jane every day, but I can't let it consume me the way it has.

It's time to take charge of my life instead of wasting each day worrying about things I can't control.

I scratch my stubbled chin, the result of not shaving for two days. I can't remember the last time I allowed my beard to grow and decide to skip a few more days just to see what it will look like. There is no way I would ever show up to work looking this unkempt.

Shit. That reminds me. I still need to call the station to request extra time off.

Wishing I'd fully stripped out of my clothes before passing out last night, I peel off my T-shirt and shorts, letting them fall to the floor the same way I did as a teenager. I can almost hear my mom's high-pitched scolding. "Lancelot David! We did not raise you to be a slob. Pick up your dirty clothes right now."

Thinking of Mom makes me remember and appreciate all she did for me while growing up. With the long hours Dad worked, she was the one I went to when I needed support. Part of me wishes I didn't argue with her about coming home for Paul's funeral. If they'd been here for me to lean on, maybe I wouldn't have screwed up with Kellie.

After a long shower, I grab my wallet, keys, and phone before walking downstairs to the kitchen. My stomach grumbles with a reminder I haven't eaten much over the past few days.

Since my parents are away, the refrigerator is basically empty. I'm grateful my mom still cooks extra-large portions and freezes the leftovers. I remove an aluminum pan of Mac N Cheese to thaw for dinner and open the last can of tomato soup. Hopefully, it will tide me over until I finish making calls and can get to the store.

Sitting at the kitchen table, I send a text to Jackson.

. . .

Lance: Hey, I just woke up. Gonna run some errands. I'll call you when I get back.

Jackson: Thanks for checking in buddy. I'll be around all day.

Lance: 10-4.

The next call is to the station to request additional time off. I was granted two weeks of leave after Paul's death, but I think I should take some extra time to get my head on straight. Generally, this needs to be scheduled months in advance, but under the circumstances, I'm confident I will be granted the time I need.

The desk clerk answers and transfers me to the administrative office.

"This is Sergeant Williams."

"Hey, Sarge, it's Deputy Malloy."

"Lance, it's good to hear from you. How are you doing?" He sounds like a concerned friend.

"Better, but not great. I'd like to take some more personal time."

"How much do you need?"

"Do you think I can take two weeks?"

"Of course, and if it turns out you need more, let me know."

"Thanks. I'm pretty sure that will be enough, but if I need to extend it, I'll call right away." The tension in my shoulders eases with the knowledge I don't have to rush back.

"Okay. I've noted it on the calendar. We will handle your shifts until you're ready to return, but don't rush. Have you been in touch with Jackson?" I guess this is his gentle nudge to peer support, which is already on my to-do list.

"Yeah, you know he wouldn't let me disappear completely." Part of me is appreciative, and the other part is annoyed that everyone assumes I need this one-on-one support.

I hear the clicking of the keys on a keyboard. "I'm sure Jackson has this already, but I just sent you a schedule of the peer meetings as well as some other resources that might help."

"I appreciate it, Sarge. I have a full day ahead of me, so I better get moving. Thanks again for the extra time off. Tell everyone I'll be back soon."

That's one call down and what feels like a thousand more to go.

Jackson's idea of staying in contact means at least two calls a day. One when I wake, and one sometime in the evening. We don't talk about Paul or what's going on in my head. Basically, he asks how I'm feeling, I say fine. Our conversation turns to something random and then I promise to call again later. It's been three days of the same routine. The next peer support meeting is this weekend. I'm nervous about attending but ready to move forward as well.

I'm usually up before the sun rises, but today it's nearly 11am when I open my eyes. I hear a noise coming from the kitchen. Cautiously, I descend the stairs and peer around corners, trying to figure out what I'm dealing with. The strong scent of garlic and the sizzle from something cooking on the stove has me baffled. A few more steps and I hear my mom's voice.

"David, do you want another cup of coffee?"

What the hell are they doing home?

"You two scared the life out of me. I thought you were in Italy for another week. What happened?" Both Mom and Dad turn to look at me.

Mom kisses my cheek and tells me to sit down at the table beside my father. "Oh, honey. Did you think we would leave you on your own right now?" She brings me a burger and fries. I guess she found what I had in the fridge for my dinner and decided it would be lunch instead.

My dad folds up the newspaper and places it on the table. "We got home around midnight. Jackson said you'd been sleeping better, and we didn't want to wake you."

"Wait. What? Why would you talk to Jackson?"

Mom wrings her hands and won't look at me. "Now, don't get mad at Jackson. He's been keeping us up to date on how you're doing. It's how we knew you were staying here."

I try to keep my cool at Jackson's interference and blatant betrayal of trust. I know it comes from a place of concern, but the constant meddling as if I can't decide for myself is beginning to wear thin. "That's not the point. He shouldn't have gone behind my back like that."

"Please don't get angry. I called him after the funeral because I was worried. I know you're a grown man, but I'll always feel the need to protect you."

I want to be furious at Jackson but can't seem to be more than just a little annoyed. I feel some relief from having my parents with me. He obviously knew something I didn't.

"Fine, but he should have told me." I squirt some ketchup, mayonnaise, and mustard onto my plate for my fries. "I'm glad to have you home. Did you enjoy your trip?"

"Yes, it was everything I dreamed it would be. I can't wait to go back and travel to all the places I have added to my bucket list. England, Ireland, and Australia have been inked onto our calendar over the next three years." Mom's excitement spills out while sharing more about her plans. "And you know, once it's inked, we can't change it."

Dad pauses mid-bite and raises an eyebrow in question. Placing his cheeseburger back on the plate, he slowly wipes his mouth. "I said, maybe we can travel to those locations."

"Dad, you can't fool me. We all know it's just another way of you saying, Yes, Dear."

We all laugh because my dad would find a way to take her to the moon if she asked.

"Anyway, your mom and I were talking this morning, and she came up with a great idea, for once." Their teasing reminds me of how much they still love each other.

"It is a great idea." She turns to me. "Remember when you and your father used to go camping and hiking in Yosemite National Park for boy scouts?"

"Umm, that's kind of random, but yeah."

"I thought it might be nice if you and Dad took a few days and did it again. You know, a father and son thing." Her smile is forced as if she's trying to hide her worries.

"Dad? Are you good with this crazy plan?"

"Yep. I could use some exercise after all the pasta and wine I had on this trip." He leans back and rubs his stomach for effect.

The more I think about this trip, the more I agree with the idea. I need to get out of this house, and I've had some questions I'd like to ask Dad without being interrupted.

"Let's do it." Feeling just a little bit lighter, I dip another fry into the mustard and listen to Mom rattle off the list of things we still need for the trip.

~

Searching through multiple boxes for camping gear in my parent's garage turns into a full day of reminiscing. Mom pretends her sniffles are from seasonal allergies, but I know she's lost in memories from long ago. The keepsake trinkets from elementary school are all stored carefully for special times just like this.

"Lance, do you remember the day you gave me this gift?" Mom holds up a misshapen, clay pinch pot bowl with feathers stuck to the sides. It was a classroom project that doubled as a Mother's Day present. Her mouth curves into a wide smile while silently reading the card I made to go along with the hideous creation.

"I can't believe you kept it. Isn't that from third grade with Mrs. Schuler?" She is my all-time favorite teacher and I'll always be grateful for the extra time she spent tutoring me when I struggled with my assignments. It's because of her that I still enjoy reading today.

"I can still picture you in your Ninja Turtles pajamas standing beside my bed proudly with a tray of rubbery eggs, burnt toast, and a mug full of hot water and coffee grounds. You were so cute trying to surprise me with breakfast in bed."

Not knowing how to use the coffee maker, I forgot to use a filter, allowing the grounds to fall into the mug. "If I remember correctly, you ate more than half that disgusting food."

"Of course I ate it. My son cooked me a Mother's Day breakfast fit for a queen." She glances over to my dad who raises a questioning eyebrow. It was an unspoken message if I'd ever seen one.

"Alright you two, what are you not telling me?"

"Okay, it's time for complete honesty. I only took a few bites while you were in the room. It's why I sent you away to get a napkin. I flushed the eggs and coffee the minute you walked out. It was awful." She wrinkles her nose and giggles.

"Mom, how could you lie to me?" I clutch my chest, exaggerating my hurt before laughing with her.

Dad chuckles and says, "Just wait, you'll do the same when you have kids. We do the best we can to save our children from being hurt even if it means a little white lie now and then."

"Speaking of children?" Mom's attempt to dig for information on my relationship status is the same as always.

Knowing where this line of questioning is going, I stop looking for the tent and wait for the interrogation to begin.

"I was just wondering if you might be seeing anyone special?" Mom bites her lip. If I had to guess, Jackson has been giving her a lot of information, and now she's playing innocent.

"Something tells me you know already and that you've been gossiping with Jackson."

"Okay, you caught us. He told me you met a woman and that you two seem perfect for each other but that it couldn't have happened at a worse time."

"Yeah, Ma, he's right. Kellie is amazing. Only I royally screwed it up."

I relay most of the events, starting with meeting Kellie and Rory over six months ago while on the job right up to the night I left town. Mom and Dad listen and remain quiet. When I get to the funeral, Dad reaches over and pulls mom into his side. I'm not sure if it were to comfort her or himself, but it was a sweet gesture that made me wish Kellie were here beside me.

"I was supposed to go back to her house when I received the letter from Paul, and I panicked."

Mom's brow wrinkles with worry. "Have you spoken to her since you got here?"

I snap the lid back on the box I was searching through

and use it as a place to sit. My intention was to talk with my dad privately, but now seems as good a time as any.

Nervously, I wipe my clammy palms on my thighs. "No, not yet. As messed up as I am, I'm not sure if I should contact her at all."

Dad removes a folding camping chair out of the nylon bag and opens it for my mom to sit beside me. He drags a storage container for himself, putting us all at eye level.

"I get the feeling that dealing with Paul's suicide is only part of your problem. How about you give us the full story so we can help?" Dad's way of getting right to the point allows me to open up.

"I'm not sure I can be the man she deserves. You both know how hard life can be with my job. What if I'm injured or worse? It's not just Kellie I need to consider. What if I can't be the father figure Rory needs?"

"Let me get this straight. You feel weak and think you aren't good enough for this woman." Is this a statement or question I wonder? "You've suddenly figured out you're not immortal because you have someone you want to love and have them love you in return. But instead of trying your hardest to be that man, you're ready to give up." Dad's comments are tough to hear but dead-on accurate and to the point.

Not sure how to answer, I sit in silence.

Finally, Mom speaks up. Her voice is low, as if she's struggling to speak. "I'm so sorry, Lance. I feel like this is my fault. If I hadn't been so difficult about you becoming an officer, you wouldn't doubt yourself right now."

"That's not true. I know why you tried to stop me, but I didn't understand the extent of it until now. I think my doubts would have appeared at some point, but Paul's death just brought it all to the surface at a time I wasn't ready for."

"I won't pretend our life is perfect. We experienced the same ups and downs in our marriage as most couples do. When the overwhelming doubts and fears snuck into my thoughts, we communicated and worked through it together." Mom wipes away the tears that have slipped down her cheeks. "If I were provided the opportunity to go back in time, I wouldn't change a thing. We love you, Lance. You are a good man and any woman would be blessed to have you by her side."

"This is just a rough spot in your life," Dad says, and I want to believe him. "It will eventually pass, and when it does, who do you want by your side?"

There's no hesitation in my answer. "Kellie. She's the only one I've thought about since I first saw her frightened and clutching Rory to her chest. I knew then she was the strongest, most beautiful woman I'd ever meet, and maybe if I were lucky, the stars would align, making her mine."

"Do you love her?" Mom looks at me with a glint of hope in her eyes.

Admitting my feelings, I softly whisper, "Yeah, Ma. I love her."

"Then tell her. Life is too short to sit around and wait for great things to happen. You need to go to Kellie and let her decide for herself if she thinks you're good enough for her and Rory." She stands, kisses the top of my head, and walks back into the house.

"She's right you know."

"You're just saying that because Mom will kill you if you disagree."

"Nope, that's not why at all. It's because that's the same speech she gave me while we were dating and I tried to run away from her."

My mouth falls open with the shock when hearing my dad had the same doubts and fears I'm having now.

"Why don't we put this camping trip on hold for another

time. It sounds like you have something more important to take care of." He stands and claps me on the shoulder. "You get to clean up out here while I help your mother with dinner."

Sitting in silence, I repeat my mom's words.

Let her decide if she thinks I'm good enough for her and Rory.

Removing my phone from my back pocket, I pull up Kellie's number and press the call button. After a few rings, I'm diverted to voicemail. Immediately my nerves kick in and sweat forms on my brow. I decide to hang up without leaving a message when the familiar tone of an incoming call stops me. Checking to see who is calling, I see the name I am simultaneously happy and terrified of right now—Kellie.

5

KELLIE

Shopping with Rory and Mom today was exhausting. My niece had another growth spurt. Everything in her closet is too small or will be very soon. This includes her favorite pink sparkle jeans that now sit above her ankles like peddle pushers. New shoes are also necessary since her feet have grown a full size in the last two months.

When we finished, mom asked if I had any upcoming plans this week and if I minded Rory spending the next few days with her and dad. They would like to get in as much Rory time as possible before settling into the newest phase of her life. Preschool begins in just a few weeks, and we agreed it's crucial to settle Rory into a schedule as soon as possible before the first day of class.

You would think I'd be doing something productive with all this alone time, but I can't seem to find my focus. Instead of finishing the monthly reports for my boss, Aaron, I've been staring blankly at my laptop screen for several minutes.

With Rory gone, I have a full list of items I should be working on, but with only the sound of my fingertips randomly striking the keys, my thoughts wander off to places better left alone.

For what feels like the millionth time since Lance left, I debate whether to wait for him to contact me or throw in the towel and call him first. I know reaching out to him breaks my promise to Jackson. He needs space, but my heart wants what it wants. Aware that making the call will be a mistake, my eagerness to hear Lance's voice has me ready to throw caution to the wind once more.

"Damn it!" I shout out my frustration to an empty house. Sorting through the reasons in my head why I shouldn't call is pointless. I push back my chair and stand tall, resolved to stop dwelling on something I know isn't good for either of us.

I need a distraction—something to wear me out, keep my mind numb, and actually accomplish something today. Scanning over my endless list of projects, I pick the ones I've been putting off and added a few of the everyday tasks just so I don't run out of things to do.

With a continuous loop of boy band music filling the air and a mop as my dance partner, I sway through a mountain of chores. In just a few hours, I succeed in completing everything on my list. Three loads of laundry, windows washed, kitchen floor mopped, and the bathrooms scrubbed from floor to ceiling. Muscles I haven't used in years scream at me to take a break as my belly growls angrily with a reminder that it's way past dinner time. Leftover meatloaf and potatoes get tossed into the oven while I pad down the hall to take a quick shower then change into something to lounge around in.

Hair twisted up in a towel, flannel sleep pants, a baggy T-shirt, and I'm set for a night of quiet relaxation. Tugging the pink throw blanket over my lap, I settle onto the couch with my dinner. After a quick search in between the cushions, I find the remote and switch on the TV.

My plan to binge on the newest *Netflix* series everyone's been raving about is interrupted by the muffled ring tone and vibrations from my cell phone. Unfortunately, I have no idea where the sound is coming from. I must have put it down while cleaning. *Where the heck did I leave my phone?*

It stops ringing before I can find it under the pile of Rory's coloring books on the table. The missed call notification shows Lance's name, causing me to choke on the potato I was chewing. I sip at my water to slow the coughing, then press the return call button.

"Oh, umm. Hi, Kellie." Lance stammers and sounds nervous, or maybe he's surprised I called.

Shit, maybe he butt-dialed me by accident and wishes I hadn't called back.

"Hi, Lance. I saw you called but couldn't find my phone before it stopped ringing. I guess you didn't mean to call me. I'll let you go."

"No. I mean, yes, I meant to call you. Wait. Don't hang up. So, umm…I know I should have called before now. I'm so sorry I left without talking to you."

"Don't be sorry. I'm not angry. You were going through so much. I can only imagine how confused you were that night. I wish I could have helped in some way."

"I'm not sure anyone could have helped me at that moment. I just needed to escape, so I did."

"It's fine. I'm glad to hear from you." My heart races, and butterflies flutter wildly in my belly, waiting for him to continue. I should be pushing him away, giving him the time Jackson spoke about and yet here I am hanging on every word he says.

"I may not have called, but you were never out of my thoughts. How are you?"

He was thinking about me. "I'm good. You know, same thing, different day. Rory's with my parents for a few days. I've done a lot of cleaning today without her around. How are you doing?" I'm rambling; my nerves ramped up to the max.

"Not perfect by a long shot, but each day is a little better than the last. Figuring out a way to accept Paul's death and move on with my life has been hard, but I'm getting there. It's what he'd want."

"I'm really happy to hear that. Listening to everyone talk about Paul after the funeral, I'm certain he wouldn't want you to remain stuck in the memories of his death."

Lance gives a hoarse chuckle and says, "You're 100% right on that. Paul's probably been trying to figure out a way to shoot lightning bolts at me with a not so gentle reminder to pull my head out of my ass."

"That sounds exactly like something a best friend would do." I laugh along with him and picture his perfect smile while we talk about Paul. I wish for more of these happy moments for Lance while thinking of his friend.

An awkward silence falls between us. If not for hearing his breathing, I would have thought he hung up. "I'm glad you called. To be honest, I almost called you myself today."

"Really? What stopped you?"

"I know you have a lot going on in your head. You don't need me adding to it. That and well, I promised Jackson I would wait for you to call me."

Lance swears under his breath. *Crap,* I guess I should have kept that last part to myself.

"It wasn't his place to tell you not to call me."

"It was hard waiting to hear from you, but I agreed because it was necessary. Remember, I went through some of this myself with Leslie and don't forget Jackson just wants what's best for you, as I do."

"You're probably right, but I still need to talk with him about his interference." He takes a deep breath and blows it out as if preparing to continue. "Anyway, I called specifically to tell you how sorry I am for how I left. You don't deserve to be treated so badly."

"No, no, please. I'm the one who is at fault. I don't know what I was thinking that night. You were grieving, and I only made it worse."

"Kellie, listen to me. You did everything right, and without you by my side, I wouldn't have survived the week. As weird as it sounds, it was because of you that I found the courage to leave, forcing me to face what is now my new reality. It was cowardly to just take off with no explanation, but I think if I'd stayed, I would have been in limbo. Just going through the motions, consumed by grief but hiding it from the outside world, same as Paul did."

"But Lance—"

"Let me finish, please. Leaving gave me the space I needed to reflect on the events that led up to Paul's suicide. But even more important, it made me look at my own life and what I want for the future."

My heart pounds and my world stops spinning. Hearing Lance speak about his future has me desiring something I cannot have. No matter what he has decided, I know he will be better off without the additional burdens that come along with dating a single parent. Although I want nothing more than to be a part of Lance's future, I need to do what's best for him.

"Look, I know I still have a lot of work ahead of me, but I don't feel like I'm carrying the weight of the world on my shoulders. I hate myself for how I acted after Paul died, and I won't lie to you and pretend I didn't use what we have between us to hide my grief, but that doesn't mean I don't have strong feelings for you. That part of us was real from the moment we met. The day I walked into your sister's apartment, you were the one. The sweet taste of your lips the night we reconnected at Heath's." He takes a deep breath, then continues. "Your silent strength while I said goodbye to Paul." I hear a crack in his voice. "Waking up beside you the next day and feeling like everything was perfect. I needed those memories to get me to where I am right now."

"I'm glad I could be there for you and don't have any regrets for the time we spent together." I bite my lip, fighting to hold back my tears. "Maybe we both made some mistakes. The timing just wasn't as right as we thought it was. Perhaps the universe was just playing a bad joke, and it was fun while it lasted, even if it was only a short time." I wish I could believe the word vomit spilling from my mouth, but it's for Lance's own good.

"Screw the universe and the supposed cosmic forces having the power to determine my future. If I learned anything over this past week, it's that we control our own destiny, not some invisible cosmic force. It's time to grab hold of my life and go after what I want most."

"Lance, stop. We shouldn't do this. You're figuring out how to live without someone who will always be important to you and I'm just trying to get by raising Rory as best I can. I got caught up in the fairytale and now reality has bitten me on the ass."

"Are you trying to say you don't have any feelings for me?" There is hurt in his question as if my words wound him.

"That's not what I'm saying at all. Yes, I have feelings for you, but that doesn't mean either of us is ready for the responsibilities a new relationship brings." *Shut up, Kellie.* "It doesn't change the path we are both traveling. You need to continue to heal while I have to stay steady for Rory. Everything I do affects her, and I can't afford to screw that up by veering off course again."

"You're right, we both have a path, but ours have crossed twice now. I agree, though. Rory should always come first. The way you care for her is just one of the reasons I..."

My heart skips when he stops abruptly. "Stop, please. You're making this harder for both of us."

"The last thing I want to do is hurt you any more than I already have." His voice softens. "Kellie, you're the only thing that makes sense in my life, and it's not to distract me from my grief this time. I miss my friend, but I miss you too. Please, don't give up on me."

Cue the tears because this man just ripped me to shreds with his admission.

"I'm not giving up. I'm giving you space. Can you understand the difference?"

He doesn't answer immediately, causing my pulse to quicken with fear. Will pushing him away only make him spiral again?

"Yeah, I understand, but before I hang up, I have just one question. I need you to think hard about what I'm asking before you give me your answer."

"Okay, sure. What's your question?" My stomach cramps with nervous knots.

"I can't see a future without you in it. I know I screwed up, but I don't want to lose you. Is there any possible way you can find forgiveness for what I've done, and maybe, sometime soon, give us another chance?"

"Oh, Lance." The protective walls around my heart have been smashed to rubble and I'm done fighting. My heart wants to scream yes, I still love you and want another chance, but he's right. I need to think this through because this decision will impact our future, but more importantly, Rory's. Although everything points to us going our separate ways as the best option for everyone right now, deep down, I can't let go of the sliver of possibility that I could be wrong.

"I'm not ready to lose you, but I'll respect your decision if you say you don't want to try one more time."

"Alright, I understand and promise to think hard about what you are asking before giving you an answer." My mind is swirling with relationship pros and cons. For the first time, Lance and I are going slow and thinking before we leap.

"Perfect. That's all I can ask. Good night, sweetheart. I will be in touch with you again in a few days, but if you need me before then, please don't hesitate to call."

The serious tone of our conversation turns on a dime when he calls me sweetheart.

"I promise I'll call if something comes up. Good night, Sir Lancelot." I giggle. He may hate the name, but for me, no matter what the future holds, he will always be my knight in shining armor.

Before I pull the phone away from my ear, I hear his chuckle. Imagining his smile makes his question just a little bit harder to say no to. But that's okay because right now, I have no intention of saying anything but yes.

6

LANCE

Sliding the last cardboard box into the back of my truck, I slam the tailgate closed and walk back into my parent's house to let them know I'm leaving. Mom insists on sending me home with all the camping gear, hoping it might encourage me to start hiking again. In reality, I think it was her way of cleaning out the garage without Dad objecting too much.

It's time to quit hiding and get back to work but more importantly, Kellie.

In the kitchen, Mom is humming a tune I don't recognize while making sandwiches. Dad appears to be engrossed in something on his laptop screen and doesn't look up.

"Well, I'm all packed and ready to go."

"Wait just a minute. I'm making you some snacks for your drive home." Mom places several plastic baggies into a large soft-sided cooler.

"You don't have to do that. It's not like I can't stop if I get hungry."

"Let her do it, son. It makes her happy."

"Yeah, listen to your father. It makes me happy and reminds me of when I used to make your school lunches."

I chuckle and kiss her on the cheek. "Thanks. Your food will be much better than anything I can pick up on the road."

Zipping up the bag, Mom then hands it to me. The weight of the cooler surprises me, causing me to misjudge and almost drop it.

"Holy cow. How much do you think I'll eat on the way home?"

"There's a frozen casserole on the bottom, so if you don't eat it tonight, make sure to stick it back in the freezer."

"What would I do without you?"

My words make her smile. "This way, I know you'll have at least one home-cooked meal this week." She loops her arm through the crook of my elbow and walks me outside. Dad follows close behind.

Standing beside my truck, mom gives me a hug and steps back. "Will you call us when you get home? I know you're a grown man, and I don't mean to baby you, but you've been through a lot, and I worry."

"I'm okay, Mom, really."

I can see she isn't convinced but isn't that a mother's job–to worry. "You do seem much better than when we first got home."

"I feel better too, and to be honest, it was nice being looked after."

"I'll always worry about you, Lance, but I don't want to be a bother."

"You're not a bother. I promise I'll call. I'm lucky to have parents who care." I lean in to kiss her cheek.

Dad hugs me and says, "We are the lucky ones."

"I better get on the road. I'm meeting Jackson later." I don't want to cause Mom to worry, so I leave out that I'm attending my first peer support meeting tonight.

This extra time with my parents has improved the relationship between my dad and me. We shared stories about what it's like to be an officer now, compared to years ago. How so much has changed, yet, it's all stayed the same.

I was shocked when he admitted there was a time he regularly attended peer meetings. Like most sons, I thought my dad was invincible. Hearing him talk about his struggles reminds me I'm not unique in suffering the emotional turmoil that has me turned inside out. It gives me hope that with help, I will get through this difficult time too.

"Bye. We love you. Be safe." Mom calls out as I slowly drive away. I watch them in my rearview mirror, waving goodbye before turning and walking back to their house hand in hand. It makes me think of Kellie and how I want that to be us in twenty years. Maybe we will be the ones waving as Rory drives off to college.

Instead of heading straight home, I decided to stop by the cemetery. This time entering through the iron gates, the sun is shining bright. It's a warm day and there is barely a cloud in the sky. The weather matches my peaceful mood. Looking around the spacious grounds of the cemetery, I only notice a few cars.

Picking up the bouquet of red roses mixed with blue iris off the passenger seat, I walk softly across the perfectly manicured lawn to the large headstone where Paul and Jane lie side by side. I inhale the sweet fragrance of antique

in full bloom lining the nearby stone walkway. I didn't notice on the day of the funeral but mixed with the scent of flowers and the serenity of my surroundings, I feel a sense of peace, something I haven't felt in a while.

Set at the end of the path is a magnificently carved white marble angel with arms open wide. Its setting couldn't be more perfect–opposite a line of benches, a serene location for family and friends to reflect upon the past with their loved ones.

Kneeling, I brush away the dry grass clippings and place the flowers beside the black granite gravestone. Etched into the top half of the stone are two entwined hearts. Words that describe my friends perfectly stab at my heart, but I focus on the important part–they are at rest, together.

Two Hearts, One Destiny

Jane Alicia Lancaster	Deputy Paul Richard Lancaster
Loving Wife and Daughter	Loyal Husband and Son
Strong, Beautiful, Fighter	Honor, Dedication, Courage

I trace my fingertips over the engraved seven-point star with Paul's badge number. Seeing his name beside Jane's has me feeling conflicted. Knowing I'll never see them again hurts like hell, but at the same time, I am relieved to know they are together for eternity.

"I miss you, man, but I get it now. You always did do things your own way." I hear the crack in my voice. "I hope you've found happiness and that you and Jane are together the way it was always meant to be."

The cemetery is still, with only a slight breeze rustling the leaves. A nest of baby birds chirping from a nearby tree draws my gaze upward. Enjoying the tranquility of this holy space, I look up to the sky, knowing Paul is watching over me.

I've shed a million tears since Paul's death, and today is no different, but I allow them to fall because freeing my emotions will set me on the path to healing. Today is about remembering my friend and how he lived, not how he died.

"Hey, remember that night I had to drop you off at home after poker, drunk off your ass, and Jane locked you out?" A smile creeps across my lips at the memory. "How I smoothed things over for you? Well, buddy, it's time to repay the favor." I notice an elderly lady clutching a bunch of flowers, watching me from afar, and offer a friendly smile. "If you have any pull with the man upstairs, now's the time. I could use some divine intervention to convince Kellie to forgive me." I watch as the lady places the flowers on a grave and wonder if she is there to visit her husband. "I've watched you work your magic on the Command Staff more than once. If anyone can get the big guy to help me out, it's you." I stand and wipe the tears from my eyes with my monogrammed handkerchief. "Well, wish me luck. I'll be by again soon. I love you both."

Sitting in the Sheriff's Department parking lot, drumming my fingers on the steering wheel, I remind myself that attending this meeting tonight is an essential step towards reclaiming that missing chunk of my life. Not only for my sake but to show Kellie I am the man she can depend on. Knowing tonight will bring out some of the memories I've pushed aside is unsettling. It's been easier to pretend they aren't there than confront them head-on.

I still have nightmares about the morning we found Paul. The blood-splattered walls, following the ambulance to the hospital, and hoping somehow my friend would survive. Perhaps those images will never leave me, but I won't allow them to taint my memories of a good man.

Sweat begins to bead on my brow and my breathing rapidly increases. Closing my eyes, I work to pull myself out from the panic attack threatening to make its way to the surface. After a few deep breaths, my pulse slows to a normal rhythm.

A light tap on my truck window draws my attention away from the dark path my mind was traveling down. "Hey, Lance. Everything alright?"

Jackson runs the meeting, so I'm not surprised he's come looking for me. We were both affected by Paul's suicide. Only he's dealing with the aftermath much better than I have so far.

Jackson opens the truck door and asks me again, "Are you okay?"

I unbuckle and climb out of the cab, closing the door behind me. "That depends on what you call okay. My best friend is dead, so I guess you could say no, I'm not okay."

I shouldn't snap at him. I'm on edge and don't have the energy to care that I'm acting like a jerk. This is just a prelude to the ass-chewing coming his way for his constant meddling. Even though a part of me understands why he butted into my business, I'm still pissed he told Kellie not to call.

"I'll let that slide because I know coming tonight isn't easy." He puts his arm around my shoulder and guides me into the station where the weekly meeting is held.

I was so deep in thought while Jackson led me into the building, I didn't notice we were in the conference room until he pulled out one of the chairs tucked under the table. "Sit down. The rest of the group should be here soon. Can I get you something to drink?"

"I'm guessing whisky isn't on the menu." Jackson quirks an eyebrow. "Kidding. Black coffee is fine. Thanks."

With my elbows resting on the table, I hold my forehead in my hands, praying these classes will help get me ready for the next stage of my life. I want to look in the mirror without berating myself for the mistakes I've made.

The ache from losing Paul is still here, but I realize now that his actions are his responsibility. From this moment on, I accept I can only control myself. Tonight, I am here for Kellie, Rory, my family, and sitting at the top of the list, me.

My fears about having to spill my guts to my friends were put to rest immediately when Jackson opened the meeting with a short prayer for all first responders and their families. I imagined the class would be set up with chairs in a circle, how support groups are often portrayed in movies and TV. Each participant introducing themselves before the group replies, "Hi, Lance."

It wasn't like that at all. In fact, it was more about listening to what others in the group shared. Jackson spoke about stress and how it is different for us with a heightened level of alertness.

Once I became comfortable and realized I wasn't alone in my emotional distress, I was able to open up. It felt great to let go of some of the anger and pain I've kept locked inside.

Jackson spoke to the group about how downtime and vacations need to be planned for our physical and mental health. His words hit home.

"We all make plans to spend time with our families, but how many of us actually follow through? Sure, banking all your vacation time seems like a smart way to prepare for the future. I bet at some point in your career, you've thought about saving your vacation and personal days so you can cash out when retirement comes around."

I know I'm guilty of doing the same thing. Thinking back,

that is exactly what my dad did for his retirement. "Did you know, by not taking time off, you could be causing yourself physical harm because your mind and body require regular breaks from this job?" Jackson pauses long enough to make eye contact with each person in the room. "I encourage each one of you to plan a trip out of town. Make some happy memories with friends and family." He allows time for his words to sink in, then he hits us between the eyes by getting to the crux of the issue. "Look, we all know our job is unpredictable. Spend time with the people who are important to you now. Don't wait for a day that may never come."

It seems Jackson's words hit home as vacations and family get togethers are planned. I even extend my own invitation to have everyone over to my place for a BBQ next month. Hopefully, this wave of enthusiasm won't fade away any time soon.

Once the meeting ends, I stay behind to help Jackson clean up. Sliding another stack of chairs to the side, my phone buzzes in my pocket. A flash of excitement that Kellie might be texting causes my pulse to quicken. Unfortunately, my wishful thinking is squashed when I see the name on my screen.

Patricia: Hi, Lance. I miss you. Please call me.

"Fuck," I growl my frustration.

She is like a hungry dog with a bone. I recognize how I screwed up by allowing her to stay with me at the hospital for as long as I did. She has it in her mind that being there for me was a positive step towards rekindling our relationship. I've tried to be nice, but kind and gentle didn't work. Neither did my blunt, "Hell, no."

"What's up? Is that Kellie?" Jackson doesn't miss a beat.

Shoving my phone into my back pocket, I continue stacking chairs. "Nope, Patricia again. The last time she called, I told her I didn't want to talk to her."

"I saw her with you at the hospital and thought you two were still friends. Guess I was wrong."

"Very wrong. Obviously, I was out of my mind to let her sit with me. Paul hated her. You remember how crazy she got after our break-up."

"Yeah, I do. And even remember the night Paul told her to stay away from you or he would arrest her for stalking."

"What are you talking about? When did that happen?" I try to think back on the conversations I had with Paul but can't remember us ever talking about him issuing such a warning.

"He never told you about the night he caught her hanging around the station parking lot?"

My brow furrows, totally unaware of the details about Patricia's past antics.

"What about the hot lunches she brought to the station every day for a week?"

"Nothing. Not a word."

"At the time, Paul asked everyone to keep it to themselves. Said he would talk to you about it later. Guess he didn't want to worry you and handled it on his own." Jackson turns off the lights, locks up the building, and we walk to the parking lot.

"That must be why I didn't see her for almost a year. The night before Paul shot himself, she was at Heath's. The same bachelorette party Kellie was at. On his way out the door, Paul warned me to stay away from Patricia." I swallow hard, thinking about our last conversation. Paul and I shared a tight brotherly hug that I remember letting go first. "When she showed up the next day at the hospital, I was too lost to think much about it. Now I've started wondering how she knew I was there in the first place."

"No idea. I know you two spoke in the hallway right before she left. Nothing seemed out of sorts."

"I don't know what to do about her. I've tried being polite, but I can't continue having her calling day and night."

"Why don't you block her number?"

"Won't work. The last time I did that, she used other phones or made it uncomfortable by showing up at my house." Patricia is skating the letter of the law, which makes it more challenging to take any legal actions.

"I'll call her once more, only this time I will be very direct and to the point about why I have no desire to have her in my life."

"And what reason is that?" Jackson's cocky smile lets me know he is fully aware. He just wants to hear me say it.

"Because I'm in love with someone else." It feels incredible to say those words out loud.

"Well, alright." Jackson's smile tells me he approves. Then he pulls his keys from his pocket and uses the button on his fob to remotely start the engine of his sleek, ice blue Dodge charger. A few long strides towards his car, Jackson turns back to me and asks, "Do you miss having a sports car?"

A year ago, I traded in my cherry red Chevy Camaro, complete with the sports racing package, for this truck. "Not anymore."

"What's that supposed to mean?" Jackson's head tilts to the side like a confused puppy.

"Because muscle cars aren't exactly the best vehicles when taking trips with your family." His smile matches mine as he drives off, leaving me standing alone in the empty lot.

7

KELLIE

Last night I became so engrossed in the new book from one of my favorite authors, I lost all track of time, reading until the early hours, telling myself just one more chapter. It was only when my *Kindle* slipped out of my hands, smacking me in the forehead, I knew it was time to shut down.

The good news, I don't have a bruise. The bad news, I forgot to set my alarm before closing my eyes, and now I'm running late. Sleeping in when Rory is with my parents for the night wouldn't be a problem, but I have plans with my friends today.

Gina and Dirk are back from their honeymoon and the last thing I need is to be late for the brunch her parents are hosting to celebrate their return.

Thank God Melanie called thirty minutes ago asking what I planned to wear. With barely enough time to shower, I told her it would be something simple.

At least I remembered to schedule *Uber* yesterday, affording me a few extra minutes to dry my hair and pull it back into a messy bun. Whoever invented this easy fashion trend needs to be inducted into the hairstyle hall of fame. Well, if there is such a thing.

While shimmying into a simple sheath dress, my phone lights up with the notification my ride is here. *Crap!* I'm later than I thought.

For a brief moment, I debate going without makeup but decide the bags under my eyes are not a good look. Thankfully, I'll have plenty of time to take care of it from the back of the car.

Walking through the open front door of Gina's parents' home, the sound of laughter coming from the kitchen makes me smile. I find my best friend talking to three middle-aged women I recognize from the wedding. She stops mid-sentence and rushes toward me.

"Kellie! You made it!" Gina pulls me into a tight hug, rocking me side to side.

"Are you kidding? I wouldn't miss your mom's mimosas for anything," I tease.

"You can't fool me. No matter how delicious Mom's cocktails are, I know you missed me." We fall away from one another as a server walks by with a full tray of drinks. She grabs two flutes filled with champagne and orange juice. Handing one to me, we clink glasses, and each takes a large sip.

"I don't know what your mom's secret is, but I could drink these all day if they weren't so deadly."

"Agreed." Gina sidesteps me as she scans the room.

"Who or what are you looking for?"

"Rory. Where is she?"

"She's staying with my parents a few more days."

"Aww." A glum expression settles on her face. "We have a surprise for her."

"How about pizza night at my house soon? That way you and Dirk can give it to her in person." Gina proclaimed herself as Rory's fairy godmother and spoils her rotten, so I'm not surprised she picked up something special while on their honeymoon.

"Perfect. I can't wait to see her little face light up when she opens the gift."

Gina excuses herself from the group of ladies she was speaking with, promising to finish her story before they leave. Tugging on my hand, she leads me outside to the same gazebo she stood in front of for her wedding. Benches are circling the inside, giving us a semi-private place to talk.

We sit and Gina turns sideways and asks the question I knew would be coming at some point. "Alright, best friend, spill it. What's going on with you?"

I wasn't expecting to do this right now but telling Gina we should wait until after the party is a waste of time. "I'm not sure where to start. So much has happened in such a short time."

"How about starting at the wedding? Mel sort of spilled the beans that Lance didn't make it, only saying he had a very good reason, but that it wasn't her story to tell."

"Really? It sounds like she's already shared quite a bit." I snort a laugh. Truth be told, without Melanie around to listen to my highs and lows while Gina was away, I would have gone crazy.

"Come on, you know you can trust me. Tell me what happened and what's going on with you two now."

"Fine." Relieved to have my BFF with me again, I don't hold anything back because I need her advice on what to do next.

"Holy shit! You've been pulled through the wringer with this man."

I gaze at the hills surrounding us and tell Gina everything. "Why would we meet up again if we weren't meant to be together. Am I just fooling myself?"

"No, I see how deep Lance has burrowed into your heart. You've always been the one who dreamed of her prince charming, but nobody ever said it would be easy."

"How do I move forward?" She shrugs her shoulders because she knows I hold the answers, nobody else. "I want the best for him, even if that means I'm not in his life." My chest tightens. It's difficult to continue. "And what about Rory? I can't think of my feelings without considering how it will affect her."

"Stop doubting yourself. Rory is happy when you are happy."

"But I promised to protect her, and right now, I'm lost between my desires and wanting to keep her life from being turned upside down." My fingers twist nervously on my lap.

"Kellie, look at me." Turning my gaze away from the scenic hills, I see Gina's eyes sparkling with excitement. "Maybe he is the one you've always dreamed of, but you'll never know if you push him away."

"Then tell me what to do..." It's not exactly a question, more a cry for help.

"That's simple...don't give up."

"Funny, that is exactly what Lance asked, for me to not give up on him."

"No, hun. I mean, don't give up on yourself."

The brunch dishes have been put away and most of the guests have left. Melanie and I are sitting in large rocking chairs on the back porch, watching the sky change slowly from burnt orange to deep red. The temperature has dropped just enough to make this a perfect spot to relax and catch up with my friends.

After saying good night to her grandparents, Gina

appears with three crystal glasses and two bottles of white wine.

"Dirk is going to Rick's apartment to shoot pool with the guys, so it's just us ladies tonight." She hands us both a glass and pours a generous amount of wine in each.

"So sad. Married less than a month and he's already leaving you home to hang out with the guys." I shake my head with mock disapproval.

"Haha. Actually, it was my idea. I love Dirk, but we've spent every minute of every day together since the wedding, and I need some girl time."

I wonder what it would be like if Lance and I were able to spend so much time together that we need a night apart.

"I almost forgot. It's time to talk about having a regular girl's night out." My circle of friends is small. Okay, so circle is a stretch since it's only been Gina for years, but now I have Melanie too. "Come on. We can be the three musketeers. It will be fun."

"I second that." Melanie slugs her wine and pours herself another full glass.

"Damn, Mel. What was that all about?" Gina's eyes widen with concern.

"What? I'm thirsty."

Gina and I look at each other and in unison say, "Suuurrrre."

"Tell us about your trip." I reach for the bottle of wine and add a little more to my glass.

"Let's just say it started a little rough." Gina tells us in detail how the TSA security officer at the airport had to inspect her carry-on bag. When she tried to explain it was her honeymoon, and he might want to take the bag somewhere private, he didn't listen. "You can imagine the look on everyone's face when he removed my black velvet bag with the assortment of naughty gifts from my bachelorette party. I've never seen a man turn that shade of red before."

"I bet the security guy will be careful going through a honeymooner's bag in the future." I make a mental note never to pack anything embarrassing in my carry-on luggage.

"Oh no, not the agent; Dirk was the one who was beet red and embarrassed." And with that, we dissolve into fits of laughter.

Gina continued to share more about their trip while Melanie and I listened attentively.

"You know, Lance's real name is Lancelot." It seems the wine has loosened my tongue.

"Holy shit. I can't believe you kept that to yourself. You really did find your knight in shining armor." Gina squeals with delight.

"I know, right?" A tinge of guilt eats away at me for betraying his secret. "But if you meet him, you can't say anything because he hates that name."

Even though Gina and Melanie promise to keep it to themselves, I have a feeling they will store that little tidbit in their back pocket for another time.

"I'm starving. Did Aunt Rachel put anything aside before the caterers left?" Melanie fills her glass with the last of the wine.

"I think there's some cake in the refrigerator. Hang on. I'll go get it." Gina grabs the empty wine bottle and hurries into the kitchen.

When she returns, her smile is nowhere to be seen, and I suspect it's because of the woman trailing behind her.

"You remember our cousin Trish?" Gina's jaw is tight and her nostrils flare.

"Hi, Trish." I remain polite, although I would prefer to ignore her.

Melanie offers a grunt and takes the cake from Gina.

"Hi, ladies. Sorry I missed the party." Trish's vile smirk speaks to her true character. She leans back, resting her elbows on the railing facing us. "I was with my boyfriend," she coos sickeningly. "He's just wonderful and all that, but even though he knew I had plans, he didn't want to let me out of bed."

"Too bad you didn't stay there," Melanie mumbles around a forkful of cake.

Trish glowers at her and continues. "I don't think I've ever been this happy. I totally get how you feel now, Gina. I think he's the one." She is such a bitch but not as clever at playing games as she likes to think she is. Her gushing and mannerisms are exaggerated to the point of ridiculousness. In fact, everything about this performance is exactly that–a performance to try and convince us her love life is all hearts and flowers. "I'm so, so lucky to have found him." Her cutesy voice makes me want to puke, and the way she twirls that strand of hair around her fingers while wearing that stupid grin on her face grates on my nerves.

I don't join in with the banter because I can't bring myself to show her I care about anything she says. Instead, I listen to this wicked woman rattle on about how great her boyfriend is in bed and how she thinks he's going to pop the question soon.

"Anyway, I wanted to drop off your gift since I had to cut out on your wedding for an emergency." Trish pulls her phone from her back pocket and smiles at the screen. "Oh, I better go. Gina, why don't you call me, and maybe we can set up a double date soon."

With a wave over her shoulder, Trish disappears from sight but leaves a bitter taste in my mouth.

"What the fuck was that about?" Melanie's eyes are narrow slits. She hates her as much as I do.

Gina and I look at Melanie and laugh. "That's what I was just about to ask. How are you related because you guys look and act nothing alike?"

"She's our spoiled, rotten cousin."

"I can think of worse words than spoiled and rotten to describe her." I am overstepping, but Trish brings out the worst in me.

"She was the first girl born after two generations of all boys, so was treated like the golden child. She got away with murder."

"Mel and I have been fighting with Trish since we were kids. She was always a troublemaker, but it became ten times worse when her mom, our aunt, left and her dad remarried while Trish was still in high school. She was the epitome of a wild child, and my uncle chose to look the other way because his perfect little girl would never do such terrible things as she was often accused of."

"Wow. So, I guess Leslie and Trish had some things in common then. It sounds like they both knew how to lie, cheat, and con their way out of trouble."

"She's a fucking bitch and I have no time in my life for her bullshit anymore." Melanie points her fork towards Gina. "You may choose to be nice because she's our cousin, but there is no way in hell I'd invite her anywhere. Dragging her away from your bridal shower hammered the final nail in the coffin." Melanie's face twisted with anger. It was good to know she was on my side. I have a feeling a pissed off Melanie is not someone you want to cross.

"How about we get back to Kellie's dilemma and how we can help her reconnect with Lance?" I'm grateful for Gina's change of subject.

"I'm not sure there is much you can do to help."

"If there wasn't, you wouldn't have brought it up," Gina added.

"My heart wants to just go with the flow, but you know that's not my way. He has a long road ahead of him before he can fully recover from the trauma of Paul's death. Plus, there is a lot to consider when dating a cop."

"There are positives and negatives in every relationship. It's no picnic attending Dirk's stuffy corporate parties, but there is no other choice. Pretending his boss tells hilarious jokes and ignoring his wife's clown makeup is just part of what I do to make it easier for my husband."

"Not exactly the same as worrying about your boyfriend getting shot at on the job or hoping his schedule won't ruin every holiday, but I know what you are getting at."

Gina reaches across the arm of her rocking chair, taking my hand in hers with a gentle squeeze. "You're right. It's not the same at all. I'm sorry for making light of it. Lance has a dangerous job."

The three of us sit in silence, sipping our wine, lost in our own thoughts. Stressing about Lance's career and the risks involved adds to the ever-growing list of concerns I have.

Preoccupied with my fears of the unknown and adding each question to my mental list, I jump when my phone vibrates in my pocket.

Lance: Hi, beautiful. Just wanted to let you know I'm home.

"Speak of the devil. He just sent a text."

"Oooh," the girls tease.

"Do you guys mind if I call him?" Holding up my phone, I show them the message.

"Are you kidding? I'd be angry if you didn't. Come on, Cuz. Let's go see if there's any ice cream to go with this cake and give Kellie some privacy." Arms linked, Gina and Melanie step inside and leave me alone on the porch.

Instead of calling, I decide to *FaceTime*. He picks up quickly. "Hi, Kellie. It's great to see you."

Holy hell. Lance looks gorgeous and I stare a little longer than I should. I can only see from his chest up, but he's shirtless. His hair is wet and longer than the last time I saw him. A casual style that is no less sexy, but I'm sure it doesn't fit the standard expected while in his uniform.

"Oh, my gosh. I'm sorry, I should have texted back." Holding my phone up in one hand, I use the other to cover my eyes. The heat creeping up my cheeks is only partially from embarrassment. Yeah, I've seen him naked, but a lot has happened between then and now.

"It's okay, hang on. Let me put my phone down and grab a shirt."

With the camera pointed up to what I assume is the ceiling, I can hear him chuckle.

"Is this better?" I'm not sure about better since he looks just as delicious wearing a white T-shirt that stretches against his broad chest.

Deciding my lustful examination of Lance's muscular physique is inappropriate, I shift my focus to his eyes. Today they appear a bright silvery-blue instead of grey, full of life and maybe even hope.

I'm tongue-tied and can't think of anything witty to say, so instead, I choose to ignore the question. "So, tell me. When did you get home?"

"Yesterday. I had a few things to take care of or I would have called then."

"I get it, don't worry."

"Then this morning, I just couldn't seem to get moving."

"There's nothing like sleeping in your own bed."

"If I remember correctly, I slept pretty sound in yours

too." His flirty smile makes my stomach flip flop. "I have some good news." The phone shifts as he sits forward.

"You do? Well, don't keep me waiting." After our last conversation, never in a million years would I expect to see Lance smiling and as content as he appears right now.

"I've been offered a special assignment as a training officer at the police academy, filling in for a few weeks. It's a great opportunity. I've always wanted to be an instructor."

"That's fantastic. I'm so happy for you."

"Sarge thinks it might help ease me back into work too." He chews on his bottom lip.

"He sounds like a smart man."

"He is and I'm grateful for how everyone has stood by me."

"People care about you, Lance."

He ignores my comment. "It looks dark. Are you outside?"

"Good observation, Deputy. Yeah, I'm at my friend Gina's. She and Dirk had a brunch to celebrate their homecoming."

"Ah, gotcha, the honeymooners." My pulse quickens as Lance narrows his gaze. "You know, you look like an angel with the light glowing behind you."

"Smooth talker." A wave of goosebumps creeps up my body.

"Are you cold?"

"No, it's perfect. It's so good to talk with you. You seem happy."

"I'm getting there. Seeing you helps." He glances downward and dips his chin slightly, making me wonder if he's self-conscious about revealing his true feelings.

"I have to admit I love it when you smile."

"It's all I do when thinking of you." His grin is infectious. "Did Rory go to the party with you?"

I love how he asks about Rory when we talk. "No, she's

with my parents again. I feel guilty leaving her with them so much, but things will change soon."

"Why would it change?"

"She's starting preschool in a few weeks."

"Wow, I can't believe she's big enough for school." I wonder how much experience Lance has with young kids.

"She's grown up a lot since you last saw her." A wave of panic overwhelms me. I've done my best to keep all thoughts of Rory meeting Lance at arm's length until now.

What if they don't get along?

What about settling Rory into a routine? Having a child is hectic at the best of times and Lance has already told me how his life is basically organized chaos.

How will Lance handle seeing the real me? A struggling single parent who is doing her best but gets overwhelmed at times. Maybe I'm worrying for nothing? He has already agreed with me that Rory's needs will always come first, but will he understand when he is faced with it daily?

"Hey. What are you thinking? You're frowning. Did I say something wrong?"

"No, you didn't say anything wrong. I just remembered a project I need to take care of." Technically not a lie. I need to figure out how and when will be the best time to introduce Lance into Rory's life.

"Oh, okay. What are your plans for later tonight?"

"Gina, Mel, and I are having a girls' night. Chick flicks, some wine, and lots of girl talk."

"If you're drinking, does that mean you are staying overnight?" He's so cute when he switches into concerned cop mode.

"Don't worry, Deputy. I'm not driving. Mel and I already agreed to share a ride home."

"Okay, good to know." He rubs the back of his neck with

his free hand. "Can you text me when you get home, so I know you're safe?"

"Aww, are you worried about me?" I'm only half-teasing. But it feels good to have somebody care about me.

"I'll always worry, just as I will do everything I can to protect you. It's part of who I am. Can you handle that?" Although it seems like a simple question, judging by Lance's pinched brow, it's a huge deal for him.

"No. It's not a problem at all. But keep in mind, it means I get to take care of you too."

He looks away from the screen and runs his hand through his hair. Shit, I took it too far, too fast. I hold my breath, wishing I could take back my words.

"Look, I know we were supposed to wait and talk about dating, but seeing you, even on my phone screen, feels right, so I'm going to ask..." There is a brief pause. "…Kellie, will you go out to dinner with me?"

"Can I be honest?" I press my hand to my chest, hoping it will slow my racing heart before it explodes with excitement.

"Always."

"I'm so glad you asked."

"Phew…I thought you were about to break my heart."

I don't know how to react to the break my heart comment, so I gloss over it. "Waiting just these few days to tell you I want to see what we can have has been killing me."

"So, you do want to see me?"

"Yes, I want to see you and have dinner."

"Great. Is tomorrow night too soon?" Lance's crooked smile and sexy dimple seal the deal.

"Nope, tomorrow is perfect." My cheeks hurt from smiling—someone who makes me feel this good can't be wrong.

"Kellie! We are set up in the family room when you finish your call." Melanie peeks around the corner of the doorway.

"Alright, give me one more minute."

"No rush. Just wanted you to know where we are." Melanie winks and slips back into the house.

"I better let you go. Have fun with your friends and don't forget to text me when you get home."

"Okay. I promise to text the minute I walk in the door."

"Night beautiful."

"Good night, Sir Lancelot."

8

LANCE

"Deputy Malloy. I'm so glad to see you." Helen, the owner of the local diner, greets me with her familiar friendly smile. She and her husband Al have owned this restaurant for as long as I can remember. Her pink dress with the white collar, apron, and matching hat screams 1950s waitress. "Choose a booth. I'll grab you a sweet tea, no lemon."

"Thanks, Helen. It's good to be back."

I make my way to the farthest corner booth. It faces the door, giving me a full view of the restaurant, including the front door, allowing me to see Kellie the moment she arrives. Passing by a few regular customers, I shake hands but don't engage in more than a quick greeting.

"Here ya go, hun." Placing the glass of iced tea on the worn laminated table, Helen takes a seat across from me. She likes to chat with her customers before taking their orders. It's also the best way for her to gather but also share the local gossip. Instead of telling tales, Helen's eyes are heavy with worry. "I'm so sorry about Paul. He was a wonderful man. Are you doing alright?"

Knowing my honest answer of how I'll never be

completely alright again isn't what she wants to hear, I stick with, "I'm doing okay. Thank you for asking."

Reaching across the table, she pats the back of my hand in a comforting grandmotherly way. "What can I get you? Today's special is meatloaf, mashed potatoes with brown gravy, and green beans."

"Actually, I'm waiting for someone." I look at my watch and see it's 5:05 pm. My heart skips. She's only a few minutes late, but my immediate reaction is there must be something wrong, or perhaps she's in danger. My second is she isn't coming, followed by chill the fuck out. She'll be here soon. "Uh, she should be here any minute."

"Alrighty. Just holler when you're ready to order."

From the small cut out window between the lunch counter and grill, Al shouts, "Order up. Let's go, woman before it gets cold." He's trying to scowl, but I can see the love in his eyes. Theirs is a game of back and forth. He knows what is coming and she doesn't disappoint.

Placing a hand on her hip, she turns around to face her husband. "I'm coming ya old coot and quit yelling. I'm not the one who's hard of hearing."

To keep me from staring at the door, I pick up one of the plastic-covered menus tucked behind the napkin dispenser. Turning the pages slowly, I start at the early riser breakfast and read each item line by line as if I don't already know the entire menu by heart.

The tinkling of the bell over the door grabs my attention. I can feel the smile stretch across my lips when I see her.

Kellie's hair is pulled back into a high ponytail. She's dressed in dark blue jeans that accentuate the curves of her hips to perfection. Her red T-shirt and running shoes complete the casual look she obviously aimed for. It suddenly hits me–this is the real Kellie; simple, comfortable, a total contrast to the woman who wore the sexy black dress and skyscraper heels at Heath's. Either way, she takes my breath away.

I stand, intending to meet her at the door but freeze when she steps to the side, revealing the petite little girl I know to be Rory. She has grown up a lot, but I could never forget her cherubic face.

Kellie glances around the diner and finally meets my gaze. Nervously, she adjusts the strap of her purse and leans down to speak to Rory, too soft for me to hear. They hold hands as they make their way toward me.

"Hi." There's a shyness to her simple hello that endears me to her even more.

"Hi. I'm glad you could make it." Leaning in slowly, I pause to gauge her reaction to me being this close. When she doesn't back away, I brush my lips softly over her cheek and whisper, "I missed you."

Stepping back, I see the blush crawl up from her neck to her cheeks.

"I'm so sorry. I didn't intend to bring Rory with me on our first date, but my parents had plans to meet with friends tonight." She sighs deeply and offers an apologetic grin. "I didn't want to cancel, and well, this is my life."

Even though I'm unprepared for this slight change in plan, I realize I'm not afraid of it happening now. It was inevitable we would meet at some point and, as they say, there is no better time than the present.

"You have nothing to be sorry about. I'm glad Rory is here." I look down and find Rory is now standing behind Kellie, cautiously peering around her legs. "Like you said, Rory is your life. If we decide to give us a try, she should be a part of it from the beginning."

"I guess you're right, but I've never introduced her to any man before. I'm not sure how it's supposed to work." I push down the surge of jealousy that hits me when she mentions another man. We haven't talked about our past relationships, and I'll admit, I'm not sure I want to.

"There's no road map to becoming a couple, but I'm pretty sure we'll get there." Crouching low, I peek behind Kellie. "Hey there. You must be Rory."

With a tiny, nervous giggle, Rory wraps both arms around Kellie's knees and hides her face.

"She's shy when she meets new people but watch out once she gets to know you. She'll never stop talking." She tries to turn, but Rory keeps a tight hold.

"It's okay. I'm glad she doesn't talk to strangers without checking first." Unwelcome thoughts of children who have been abducted enter my mind. The idea of someone harming Rory has my protective instincts on high alert.

"Rory, this is my friend Lance. Can you say hi?" Kellie stands still while we wait for Rory to make the next move.

Still clutching her aunt's leg, Rory slowly tips her head just enough so I can see her eyes. A tiny step to her left, and I see her button nose. Another step and I'm graced with a toothy smile that lights up her whole face.

"Hi," she says in a shy whisper.

"It's nice to meet you, Rory. I'm glad you came to dinner. Are you hungry?"

She nods her head enthusiastically. "Yes."

"Me too." I raise to my full height. "Shall we sit down and you can order anything you want?" Maybe I made a mistake there, but it might help Rory feel more comfortable.

Looking to Kellie for her approval, I'm relieved when she smiles brightly. "Wow, anything you want, Rory. How does that sound?"

"Ice cream?" Rory looks up and my heart melts.

Kellie smiles and says, "Okay. Just this once."

Thankfully, I sense a slight shift in Rory. Although wary, kids can be so easily won over, and while I know Kellie would give her life for this little girl, I am not surprised to find I care so much for her too. I have never forgotten the day I saw her, surrounded by filth and parents that didn't deserve the joy of children.

Once we are seated, Kellie moves the menus, condiments, and napkins out of Rory's reach. I watch intently as she reaches into her purse and pulls out a clear bag filled with plastic animals.

"Ready?" Kellie get's Rory's attention by holding up a toy. "What's this one."

"Elephant." Rory swings an arm in front of her face and trumpets.

I bite my lip, trying not to laugh at her silly attempt to sound like an elephant.

Kellie glances my way with a smirk and keeps going. "And how about this one?"

"Piggy. Oink, oink." Rory's nose wrinkles with each snort.

"Very good. Do you remember what this guy is called?"

With her hands up, she curls her fingers into what looks like claws and shouts, "Tiger. Roar!"

"You're right." The two of them pretend to paw at each other, breaking into a fit of contagious giggles.

My laughter mixes with their squeals of delight, drawing a few looks from the other diners. They smile our way, seeming to enjoy the happy sounds floating around the room.

A sudden chill runs over my body, followed by a ringing in my ears. Shaking my head to stop the annoying sound, my breathing falters when I hear Paul's voice clear as a bell. *If she's the one, hold on tight and don't let go.* The same words he spoke just before leaving Heath's.

My eyes dart around the room, searching for anything to explain what I just heard, but nobody else is nearby. I've never believed in ghosts or signs from beyond and dismiss it as my mind playing tricks on me.

I am soon entranced by Rory. She has her arms wrapped around Kellie's neck, peppering her cheeks with a thousand kisses. The unconditional love Kellie feels for her niece is plain to see.

And that's all it took. This moment in time will be engraved in my memory forever. My fate has been sealed and there's no turning back. I want to feel happiness like this every day for the rest of my life. But not with just anyone, with Kellie and Rory. Am I scared thinking about a ready-made family? Hell yes, but it doesn't outweigh the exhilaration I feel watching Kellie interact with Rory right now. I imagine myself existing in their world.

The kisses have stopped, and Rory has turned her attention back to her toys. Kellie chews on her bottom lip while I continue to stare. I need to pull myself together and think about what my next move should be without freaking her out.

"Sorry. As you can see, we are working on animal names and sounds." Seemingly content, Rory ignores us. With the pig in one hand and a zebra in the other, she hums while walking them along the tabletop.

"I can't believe how much she's grown. That day, at your sister's apartment, she seemed so little and helpless."

"Honestly, I try not to think about it much. It's the future that matters the most."

"There's that word again."

Kellie's brow wrinkles. "What word?"

"The big F word." Utter confusion is written all over her face. "You know, future."

"Oh right, that F word." Kellie picks up a menu, flips through the pages quickly, then places it back on the table. It seems she's just as flustered over what possibly lies ahead.

There's an uncomfortable silence between us. I try to formulate my words into the questions that have been floating through my mind. Just when I think I know what to ask, Helen walks over to our table.

"Kellie, it's so good to see you and Rory again."

"Oh, hi, Helen."

"How long have you and Lance known each other?" Helen hands over a booster seat for Rory then slides in to sit beside me. I shouldn't be surprised that she knows Kellie. Helen never forgets a face and everyone in Springhill county eats at this diner at one time or another.

"Nice to see you too. Rory, look who's here."

"Hi, Helen." Rory waves shyly before picking up two more animals from the table. She has most of them lined up on the top of the leather booth, but the elephant won't stand upright. "Addy K, help me, please."

"How about we put them back on the table so we can get ready for dinner?"

"Okay." With a mischievous grin, she lifts her arm and knocks all the toys to the floor in one swoop.

Kellie's eyes widen. "Rory, that's not okay." She doesn't yell the way I've heard parents do when their kids act up. She's stern but not mean. Even with my lack of experience with kids Rory's age, I know this is normal behavior. I step away from the table and help pick up the animals while Kellie places them back into her purse. "Now, I need you to please sit down and be a good girl, or no ice cream."

Rory doesn't like being scolded, that much is evident from the sniffles and tears in her eyes. Her sad face pulls at my heartstrings in a way I don't completely understand. Maybe it's the memory of her sobbing the first time I saw her. All I know is, I would do anything to make this little girl happy.

"We've only been friends for a short time." I decide to answer Helen's question while Kellie whispers to Rory.

"Gotcha, friends." She gives me an exaggerated wink. *Just great.* The gleam in Helen's eyes means the local gossip will soon include news about Deputy Malloy and Kellie Bryant.

"Kellie, do you know what you and Rory would like to order?" Hopefully, my change of subject will keep Helen from asking any embarrassing questions. She can be ruthless when trying to sniff out a juicy story.

"Rory, do you want spaghetti or a hamburger?"

"Hambburber." On a dime, the mood is back to playful when Rory answers energetically. Her mispronunciation of hamburger melts me.

Kellie chuckles but is quick to correct Rory's pronunciation. "No matter how many times we practice pronouncing hamburger, it always has extra b's."

"Or she's got your number and knows it makes you laugh. She's a smart cookie." Helen looks at Rory. "Do you want fries?"

"Yes!" Rory doesn't hide her excitement.

Kellie places her finger to her lips and softly shushes her. "Remember we're inside and have to talk softly. You need to say yes, please."

"Yes, please," Rory repeats in barely a whisper.

Helen scribbles on her order pad. "That's one hamburger with fries, and how about you, Kellie?"

"I'll have a cheeseburger, fries, and sweet tea. Oh, and a glass of milk for Rory, please."

Helen nods. "Lance?"

"I'll have the same."

"Got it. I'll be right back with your drinks." Kellie sets a coloring book with only two crayons in front of Rory. Red and green.

"Why only two colors?"

"Oh, I learned that one the hard way. You saw what just happened with the animals. Now picture that same move with a table full of crayons. Less is sometimes more in Rory's world."

"Makes sense." I make mental notes of these little details for another time.

Kellie huffs out a breath. "So, you're finally seeing the real me. I don't wear fancy dresses unless I have to. I work from home, so sometimes I don't even get dressed until after lunch. When Rory has a good day, I feel like a superwoman. On the rare bad days, I am wiped out and just want to give up, but it's not an option. Rory needs me to keep going, so I suck it up and move on." She stops talking and stares into my eyes. Her expression is unreadable. "Are you sure you want to do this?"

There it is. The real question that has been looming between us from the beginning. Reaching across the table with both hands, I turn them palm up and wait for Kellie to accept my offer. Tentatively she slides her palms on top of mine.

"Honestly, I've never wanted anything more, but I'm terrified." She pulls her hands away, placing them back in her lap. "I'm screwing this up again. I'm trying to say I'm afraid I'm not good enough for you or Rory."

"You're wrong. You are good and kind. I watched your friends and listened to the things they said about you when you weren't around. If anything, I'm afraid I'm the one lacking and can't give you what you deserve from a relationship."

"And what is it you think I deserve?" I sit back, feeling a little deflated, and wait for her to answer.

"This isn't easy." I follow Kellie's gaze over to where Rory is sitting quietly like the perfect child. "My life isn't my own. I made a promise to my sister, and I won't betray her even in death. I'm afraid I'll fall so hard, I'll lose my way. I can't be distracted and forget my number one job is to raise Rory."

"Did you promise your sister that you would give up living? How about finding love? Was that part of the deal, that you have to do everything by yourself?" My voice is low and harsher sounding than I mean it to be, but I refuse to accept her reason for pushing me away.

"Of course not." Her eyes shine with unshed tears. "But I don't know how to do both."

"Then let me help you figure it out. I messed up by running away instead of talking to you. My guilt over the part I played in Paul's suicide consumed me just as I suspect you are still holding on to some from your sister's death. Neither Paul nor Leslie would want us to stop living." I place my palm on Kellie's cheek, using my thumb to brush away the single tear that escaped. My tough girl has a soft, vulnerable side she hides from the world. It's my job to let her know she's not alone and will never have to hide her feelings from me ever again.

When she leans into my touch, I continue. "I have no doubt I will make a million mistakes, but the one thing I can promise you is I'll never run away again."

I glance over to Rory. She's drawing big red circles over the entire page. It's messy and entirely outside of the lines, yet in my eyes, it's a masterpiece.

She remains silent. I'm not sure if she is on board or not, but my stubborn side says to keep going as if she is. "Here's how I see it. Saying we are going to start over is silly. We are far too deep into this relationship to go backward. But what we can do is move forward, communicate, and see where this goes."

Rory stops coloring and looks at me, then ducks under my outstretched arm to sit in Kellie's lap. Now I have two sets of eyes on me while I pour out my heart. "I want you in my life, and that includes Rory."

Kellie closes her eyes, and for a moment, I think she's going to reject me. When she opens her eyes, the tears stream down her cheeks. The corners of her lips tug upward into a dazzling smile. "I want that too." I hand her a napkin to wipe away her tears.

Curiously, Rory twists around to face her aunt. "Addy K, don't cry." Taking the napkin from Kellie's hand, she swipes at the tears in the same way I imagine Kellie does when providing comfort. Seems our little Rory is just as protective and caring as her aunt. Now it's my turn to take care of and protect them both.

Rory gently lays both hands on her aunts' cheeks before placing a loud, sloppy kiss on her forehead. Leaning back, Rory tilts her head and asks, "All better?"

"Yeah, you made me all better." Kellie wraps her arms around Rory, squeezing tight but keeps her eyes on me, and repeats, "You made me all better."

9

KELLIE

A tiny part of me feels guilty for being deceptive about my ulterior motive for bringing Rory on our date. I didn't completely lie about my parents being busy. When I asked them to take Rory for the night, they reminded me they had plans with friends. I could have canceled or asked Gina to come over to care for Rory, but I thought by bringing her along, I would determine if Lance was ready for what my life is really like.

My conscience knew it was unfair to test him this way, but at the time, I felt it necessary to put my mind at ease. I almost backed out of the date, sitting in the parking lot for ten minutes debating whether I should text Lance and cancel or go through with a plan that most likely would scare him off.

I should have known better because Lance isn't the type to be easily scared. He says what's in his heart without pulling punches. His honest declaration of intent toward me was a turning point in our relationship.

Requiring a moment to compose myself, I take Rory to the bathroom to wash up before eating. A quick splash of cold water to my face does the trick. I smile to myself when I hear her humming while washing her hands. To my amusement, she's singing about bonking a bunny on the head and being changed into a goon by the blue fairy. She turns off the faucet and grabs a handful of paper towels from the dispenser.

"A goon, huh?" I hold the door open for her to lead the way.

"Yep. Bonk." She pretends to hit her forehead. "I'm a goon."

I shake my head and follow my niece as she skips back to where Lance is waiting.

Ever the gentleman, he stands when we return to the table.

"Are you okay?" His eyes show concern.

"I'm fine, just needed a minute to collect myself." Rory scrambles into the booth and shoves fries in her mouth. "Slow down, or you'll choke."

With a mouthful, she gives me a big toothy smile and mumbles, "Okay."

Lance and I both laugh and dig into our own cheeseburgers.

After a few bites of her burger, Rory has overcome her shyness and bombards us with silly questions.

"Are tigers real?"

"Yeah, tigers are real." He looks at me quizzically.

I know exactly where this is going and sip my iced tea to keep from laughing. She went through this same line of questioning with my dad yesterday. Rory has developed her own sense of humor that nobody understands yet, but her. She cracks herself up, and I go along with it, glad to hear her talking in complete sentences.

"Are lions real?"

"Yes. Lions are real too." Lance looks lost, but I think this trial by fire is perfect. A little taste of what he's signed up for.

"Are ligers real?" Her eyes squint like she's trying to read his thoughts.

He doesn't hesitate. "Of course, ligers are real. They are awesome."

His confidence is just about to get crushed by a little girl.

Rory bursts into a fit of laughter. "Duh, ligers aren't really real." With that bit of knowledge, she was off, explaining how people made ligers and how you can only find them in cages, not in the wild.

"Narwhals are real and live in very cold water." She wraps her arms around her belly and pretends to shiver.

"Are you sure?" He looks to me for help, but I refuse to bail him out. She still has one more bit of knowledge to share.

"Yep. They are like unicorns but in the ocean." And now the class is over. Professor Rory has spoken and resumes eating her dinner.

Lance appears stunned as he stares at the little teacher who just schooled him in her Animals 101 class. "I honestly thought ligers were real and narwhals were fake."

"Nope. She's obsessed with the new *National Geographic* books I've been reading to her at bedtime. The latest was about animal facts vs. myths."

"Wow. I'm just amazed at how much her speech has improved in such a short time."

"She's a lot better, but I still need her to repeat herself and slow down. It's like she's trying to make up for lost time. Her speech therapist couldn't believe how quickly she progressed. You seem to understand her without any trouble at all."

"Well, that's because she's easier to understand than some of the people I take reports from."

"I can only imagine what you see daily."

"It's not all bad and even when it is, sometimes wonderful things come from it." He reaches across the table, taking my hand in his. "You've done such a great job taking care of her, just like you promised."

"Umm…" Rory interrupts. She stands on the seat, cups her hands around her mouth, and whispers into my ear. "What's his name again?"

I copy her and stage whisper, "Lance, and guess what?

"What?" Her curiosity piques.

"Lance is a deputy."

Rory's eyes widen. "Like Mr. Deputy Bear?"

Lance nods. "Yep, I am, and you can call me Lance if that's okay with Aunt Kellie."

She twists her face and wrinkles her nose like she's testing different names in her head. Finally, her face lights up, and she proclaims, "Today, I'll call you Lance."

"Tomorrow, who knows what your name will be. She likes giving people nicknames."

"Um, Lance." I am thrilled to see Rory interact so comfortably with him. It reassures me that I made the right choice in bringing her to dinner instead of canceling our date. "Can I have ice cream, please?" She points to her half-eaten burger.

"I think we should ask Aunt Kellie." Lance looks to me for help.

"Oh. My. God. I can't believe she's trying to sweet talk you already." Watching Rory play innocent is entertaining but makes me think she's going to twist him around her pinky in no time. "Not yet. You need to take three more bites and two more drinks of milk, then if you're still hungry, we will talk about ordering ice cream."

Rory crosses her arms and pouts. Over these past months,

I've become immune and silently wait for her to realize I'm not backing down.

Lance surprises me with his creative way of getting Rory to finish her meal. "Uh, oh. I better eat my dinner too, or I might not get ice cream either." He makes a show of taking a big bite and Rory copies him with a bite of her own burger.

The playful competition does the job and Rory eats everything on her plate.

"I'm impressed. It usually takes more convincing than that."

"My dad played that game a lot with me when I was a kid. He challenged me to do a lot of things when I didn't want to do them. I hoped it would work."

"Well, your instinct was spot on." I take Rory's empty plate and place it on top of mine.

Helen stops beside our table with a cart used to carry the dirty dishes into the kitchen. "Do y'all want some dessert tonight?"

Rory looks to me and I nod, giving my approval. "Yes, please." She's extra sweet and polite when she knows it will get her what she wants.

"Rory will have a small scoop of strawberry ice cream with whipped cream and I'll have a hot fudge brownie sundae."

"I'm pretty sure I know what Lance wants." She winks at me. Does she mean dessert or something else?

"Yep, same as always. I'll take a chocolate banana milk-shake. Thanks, Helen."

"You got it. I'll be right back." She pushes the cart into the back and shouts our order to Al loud enough for the entire restaurant to hear. Maybe her hearing is a little worse for wear after all.

The bond between Lance and Rory I first witnessed in Leslie's apartment was solidified over dessert.

Lance shared a childhood story about how he and his dad would order a milkshake after boy scout meetings. When Rory asked for a taste of his shake, she decided she loved it and asked if he wanted to trade. With those puppy dog eyes pleading for Lance to switch, he was a goner. Without hesitation, he slid the large glass over to Rory.

She used the long skinny spoon to scoop some of the ice cream from the bottom just as Lance had but was unsuccessful, spilling some on her shirt and dribbling more down her chin.

A few bites later, Rory looks across the table to Lance. "Want some?" There were two straws. She points one at Lance and sips from the other.

Trying to be stealthy, I snap a picture of Lance and Rory sharing their shake. Their foreheads almost touching while they each sipped from their straws was too good of a moment to miss. Lance caught me but only grinned around the straw.

Is it too much to hope my world will always be filled with this much joy?

~

Tonight has been one of the best of my life, and although I didn't want it to end, I knew I was pushing my luck expecting Rory to remain under control for so long. After a quick kiss on my cheek, a tiny wave to Rory in the backseat, Lance closed my car door and made me promise to call when I got home.

Once home, I sent a quick text letting him know I'd call when Rory was settled for the night.

Right now, it's bath time, and she is a mess.

"How did you get chocolate in your hair?" I hand her a

washcloth to cover her eyes and pour a cup of water over her head. "You're supposed to eat dessert, not wear it."

"I did eat it. Yummy." She rubs her chubby belly. "Lance shared with me."

"That was very nice of him." Using my fingers on Rory's scalp, I lather up the shampoo.

"Is Lance our friend?" This is a big question. Being someone's friend is very special for a preschooler and holds a lot more weight than it does for an adult. It's a sign she is accepting him into her world.

"Yes. Lance is our friend."

"Okay. Where's my duck?"

Her attention turns on a dime from friends to searching for her toy without a second thought. If only my life was this simple.

With Rory tucked into bed, I change into my baggy nightshirt, grab a cup of tea, and settle into my couch to *Facetime* with Lance.

"Hi, Kellie."

"Hey."

"You got Rory in bed already? I wasn't expecting to hear from you until later."

"She's already fast asleep, which surprises me with all the sugar she had today."

"I'm sorry. I probably shouldn't have told her she could have anything." He scrunches his face with worry.

"It's fine. If I wasn't on board with your plan, I wouldn't have agreed. She doesn't like being told no, but she's learning that she doesn't always get her way."

"Just add that to the list of things I need to work on to help you with Rory."

"It's a long list, but you'll catch on. Then the minute you think you've got it handled, the rules change."

"Oh, God. I am going to be terrible at this." He groans and rubs his brow. "Maybe I should start apologizing now for the millions of mistakes I know are coming." I laugh at the look of defeat on his face.

"I have been Rory's guardian for over six months now. She's happy, healthy, and growing up exactly as she should. The number of mistakes I've made already is staggering. I stopped stressing too much about them and just try to do better next time."

"If you say so. You're the expert here."

"Definitely not an expert." He's trying so hard to be the man we need.

"Oh, remember I told you about filling in at the academy for a while?"

"I remember. Is that soon?"

"Yeah, next week. It feels weird to have a Monday through Friday schedule after all these years of rotating days off."

"I bet, but maybe you'll get caught up on some sleep for a change."

"That would be nice."

"Hang on a second." Rory's door opens. "Addy K." She runs down the hall and climbs into the chair beside me. I lift her onto my lap so she can see Lance on the screen.

"It's Lance." She tilts her head and smiles up at me.

"You're right." I pull the blanket up over her. She leans back into my chest and pops her thumb into her mouth. She's tired but still wired from our exciting day. I can relate. "Now, why are you out of bed?"

"Not tired."

"Hi, Rory. I had so much fun today. Maybe I can take you and Aunt Kellie on a picnic soon." He sounds excited.

"Yes! With Jelly sandwiches?" She's fighting to keep her eyes open now.

"Sure. Anything you want."

"You might want to think about taking that phrase out of your vocabulary before you end up buying a P-O-N-Y."

"Shit. I mean shoot. It's tough to look into those eyes and ever think of telling her no."

"But you'll have to at some point."

"Promise you'll tell me if I'm screwing things up."

"Deal. But just so you know, I was exactly like that but soon found my little con girl was playing me for a fool. She's not as innocent as you think." Rory's thumb has slipped out from between her lips.

"It looks like she's asleep." His voice is soft.

"Yeah, I better get her back to bed. Good Night."

"Okay. Sleep well and I'll call you tomorrow."

Instead of carrying Rory to bed, I take advantage of the extra time to cuddle. I won't have this forever. Watching Lance with Rory was better than I anticipated. First, he stole my heart, and now he's holding a piece of Rory's too.

My breath catches as a wave of unwanted doubt swirls through my mind. I hate how I can't just live in the moment and always seem to seek out the negative side of life.

It dawns on me I've done exactly what I said I wouldn't. I've allowed Lance to break through the protective barriers. Not only am I at risk of getting hurt again, but Rory is vulnerable too. If this doesn't work, or he changes his mind, where does that leave us? Breaking my heart is one thing, but how do I keep him from breaking Rory's?

Lance said he wouldn't, but life is never that easy. I'm confident he would never do it on purpose, but after everything he's been through, I wonder if it's a promise he can actually keep.

10

LANCE

Dripping with sweat, I peel off my workout clothes and head to the showers in the men's locker room at the academy. The last two weeks working as a substitute training officer have been emotionally fulfilling. Passing along my real-world experiences and the required textbook knowledge to the recruits reminded me why I decided to join the force in the first place. More importantly, it made me appreciate where I came from and acknowledge the officer I've become.

I thought the regular hours of teaching would afford me more time with Kellie, but between the exhaustion from intense physical training and preparing for classes, we've only communicated through quick calls and text messages. I don't remember being this worn out after my own academy training, but then again, I was seven years younger than I am now.

Today was the last chance for several of these men and women to complete the grueling obstacle course within the required time limit, or they would not graduate.

Memories of Paul's struggles while trying to conquer the course is my motivation to ensure each of these recruits passes. The additional training from me and my fellow instructors paid off. For the first time in our academy history, every recruit passed and will be standing proudly, side by side, at their graduation ceremony.

Dressing quickly, I toss my things into a bag and walk to my truck. I check my phone and cringe when I see the number of messages I've missed. Unfortunately, most are from Patricia. I thought ignoring her would send the message I'm not interested, but she's worse than before. I block her number and hope she gets the message to stay out of my life.

Continuing to scroll, I stop when I get to a selfie of Kellie and Rory. This is what my future looks like. I send a quick text letting her know I'm on my way home.

Lance: I love this picture.

Kellie: Rory wanted to send it.

Lance: It made me smile.

Kellie: Then she achieved her goal.

Lance: I'm driving home now.

Kellie: Are you still up for movie night at my place?

Lance: I wouldn't miss it for the world. I'll pick up pizza on my way. I should be there in a few hours.

Kellie: Perfect. See you then.

As I approach my house, I see a familiar car in my driveway. Patricia is leaning against the driver's side door, posing in what I can only guess she believes makes her look good. All I see when I look at her is desperation.

Parking on the street, I glare at her as I climb out from my truck. The metal-on-metal crash as I slam the heavy door closed causes her to wince. I'm not trying to hide my anger. In fact, I hope the noise lets her know exactly how pissed off I am.

"Hey stranger," she purrs.

"Why are you here, Patricia? Or is it Trish today?"

"I will always be Patricia to you, but I go by Trish to everyone else now."

"Whatever. It doesn't matter since I won't be calling you anything. Hurry up and tell me what you want so you can leave."

"I wanted to see you."

"I told you to stay away." My chest is heaving with each frustrated breath I take.

"You haven't returned any of my calls or texts and I was worried something might have happened to you."

"That's bullshit and you know it. Look, I've moved on with my life, and I suggest you do the same."

"What do you mean?"

"Don't play innocent. You know damn well I'm dating someone and the last thing I need is you causing trouble for Kellie and I."

"I had no idea you were seeing anyone, Lance."

I'm not trying to be cruel, but I need her to understand I'm serious, and her behavior is out of line. "Bullshit."

I hate to use the word stalking because of the severity of the crime, but going by the letter of the law, that's exactly what she is doing.

"I don't understand. I thought we were…"

"You thought we were what?" I close my eyes and silently count to ten. "Look, I told you how I felt the last time you showed up here uninvited. You need to leave me alone. I mean it."

"But Lance…"

"Stop! I'm tired of listening to your lies. This is your last chance before I file a restraining order. You already know how that process works. I was trying to keep you from going to court and potentially spending time in jail."

"Okay, I got it."

"There is a God." Can it be this easy?

"I thought this was just another bump in the road between us, but now I see I was wrong." She shifts her weight from side to side. "You won't have to file anything. I promise to leave you alone." Her eyes well up with tears, and for a moment, I feel guilty for being so heavy-handed.

I search deep within myself for the learned skill I use while on the job to stay calm and in control. A cleansing breath to refocus my thoughts is followed by two steps back from where Patricia is standing. It gives me the necessary physical and mental space to push my emotions aside and assess the situation in its entirety.

There was a time I cared for her deeply. Not the same way I care about Kellie by any stretch of the imagination. Still, she was important to me, and my parents would be disappointed to know I was hateful to a woman who obviously needs professional help.

Over the months we dated, she shared stories from her childhood and the tough times she had when her mom left. Her father remarried and she was basically left to raise herself when a teenage girl needs her mom the most.

Her father's idea of love was to throw money her way when she acted up, providing no boundaries for her behavior. There were other parts of her childhood she refused to share. I suspect something so terrible happened she couldn't bear to dredge it up. It does not excuse her behavior, but there is a real reason for why she is so messed up.

"I hope you are telling the truth this time."

"I mean it, Lance, I swear."

"And please think about getting some help. You've been out of control for too long." My words wounded her, but it was the truth. "Your behavior at Heath's and now showing up unwelcome at my home has put me in a position I don't want to be in, but it seems to be the only thing to make you realize you've crossed the line, and now you're breaking the law."

"You're right. I'm sorry I've been such a monster. I don't know what's wrong with me." She hangs her head and I see her tears fall to the concrete.

There's a small part of me that feels bad I've hurt her. It doesn't change the message, but my delivery has been harsher than I intended. Something inside says I need to try and soften the blow, that she can't handle the brutal truth.

"You're not a monster, but you do need to talk to someone."

"I'll try. Umm, I better leave, but if you ever need anything..."

"Goodbye, Trish." I deliberately use her nickname when cutting her off.

With my arms crossed over my chest, I stand behind my truck and wait until her car's taillights are no longer visible.

Entering my house, I get the feeling something is wrong or is out of place. I've learned to listen to my intuition, but I can't place my finger on what it means this time. Perhaps it's just the frustration and anger still stirring inside me about Patricia showing up here out of the blue.

My gut tells me she won't stay away for long and that a report should be made to document her unusual behavior. Jackson should be on duty, and since he knows the history between her and me, I decide to call him to start the paperwork.

~

The drive to Kellie's gave me just enough time to shake off my shitty mood and find the excitement I felt earlier when thinking about seeing my girls.

Jackson gave me the report number for my official complaint against Patricia. It's not a formal stalking allegation but documenting her harassment. It's my word against hers, but it's how the system works. I'd be stupid to not start the process of compiling evidence just as I'd advise anyone making a similar claim. It's necessary should things go from bad to worse, and in my experience, that happens more often than anyone wants to think about.

Balancing two large pizza boxes in one hand and a bag of snacks in the other, I walk up the path to Kellie's porch. Before I can knock on the door, it swings open quickly, banging into the inside wall.

"He's here!" Rory shouts.

"Rory, you know you're not allowed to answer the door by yourself. What if it wasn't Lance?" I'm glad Kellie is firm while correcting what could have been a terrible accident.

"I'm sorry, Addy K." Rory looks up to Kellie, who swoops her up into her arms.

"I just don't want anything bad to happen to you. We need to be careful and follow the rules, okay?"

"Okay." Rory's smile has faded slightly.

Learning to be safe is crucial, but seeing her sad eyes doesn't sit well with me. Not that I disagree with Kellie's handling of the situation. I'm glad she is teaching Rory about stranger danger, even in her own home.

"I have pizza. Pepperoni and sausage for me and plain cheese for Rory. And…." I hold up the plastic bag just out of her reach. "…a special surprise for when we watch the movie."

"Yay! Surprise! Can I see?"

"Not yet. It's for after dinner."

Kellie sets Rory back on her feet and steps aside for me to enter.

"She's going to turn me grey before my time." She shakes her head and lets out a small chuckle. "What did you bring besides the pizza?"

"That, Ms. Bryant, is for me to know and you to find out."

I set the pizza boxes on the dining table and watch as Rory skips down the hall away from us. "Where is she running off to?"

"Probably to grab more pillows off my bed to toss on the floor for our movie night."

"Hmm, sounds like it's the perfect opportunity for me to steal a kiss then."

"I think we should have a minute or two before she comes back."

Kellie doesn't wait for me to make the first move. She slides her hands up my chest and stands on tiptoe, touching her lips to mine in a soft, barely-there kiss.

My body responds to the innocent brush of her lips, causing my hard cock to press painfully against my zipper. It feels like it's been years since we were last together.

The faint floral scent of her perfume is intoxicating. Or maybe it's just Kellie in my arms again that has my head spinning and heart pounding. My control is stretched thin. I need more than just a simple kiss. I want to pour every ounce of my desire into the small amount of time we have right now.

"I missed how it felt to have your arms around me." She rests her arms on my shoulders. Her fingernails trace small circles on the back of my neck before I feel them rub what little hair has grown back after clipping it short to meet the academy appearance standards. "With your hair cut so short, it's prickly. I like how it feels."

One simple touch from Kellie and goosebumps cover my body. I hold back a groan of pleasure, remembering this is just a stolen moment with a time limit. Quickly, I switch gears.

Taking her into my arms, I dip her back slowly as though we are lost to a dance.

Pausing, I look deep into her eyes, hoping they reflect the

same desire and passion I feel. "I missed everything about you."

There is no build up to this kiss–full of urgency and hunger like I've never known. Crushing my lips to hers, it's rough and demanding as our tongues meet.

Kellie claws and pulls at my shirt but with a quick tug, her body is pinned to mine. Our lips barely part as we both demand as much from the other and vie for control.

Panting, I pull back slightly and whisper, "We need to stop." I hate the words that leave my mouth.

"Okay, but you may need to carry me to the couch. My legs are like jelly." As much as she tried to control it, a chuckle comes out breathier and sexier than it should.

The sound of little feet approaching has us stepping apart like teenagers who were just caught by their parents. Rory's dragging two large body pillows behind her.

"So, this is what it will be like? Little eyes and ears spoiling our fun."

Kellie's face falls, her eyes cast down. "Umm, yeah. I guess so. Does that bother you?"

"No. Why would you think that?"

"I don't know. I just keep wondering why you would want to be with me and not some hot single woman who can go out on real dates that don't include a preschooler tagging along."

As Rory continues setting up the room, I watch as she carefully arranges the pillows in a half-circle in front of the television.

With fingertips under Kellie's chin, I tilt her head slightly. I hate that I put that sad look in her eyes. "I'm sorry. I was trying to be funny, not fill your head with doubt."

"It's not your fault. I wish I could live in the moment and stop worrying about all the what ifs of everyday life."

"You know there are good what ifs. What if the sun is

shining tomorrow and we spend a fun-filled, memorable day at the park? Or what if Rory grows up to be a doctor who discovers the cure for cancer. My point is that not all what ifs are bad." I plant a kiss on her forehead, the tip of her nose, and then her lips. "You need to stop worrying. I'm not going anywhere. Got it?"

"Yeah, I got it." She offers a weak smile.

Her short answer and soft tone tell me she doesn't completely believe me. That's fine for now. It just means I must work harder to make her see I'm in this for the long haul.

11

KELLIE

"That blanket is too heavy; it's going to fall," I warn.

"It'll be fine, trust me," Lance argues.

I knew better because Rory and I have done this many times. She knows exactly where every chair, pillow, and blanket belongs. "We'll see."

"This goes there," Rory points, providing Lance with directions on building the blanket fort.

"Here?"

"Yes."

It's just the warm-up act for our movie night. Rory eyes him with curiosity while I wait for the inevitable collapse because no matter how many times my wonderful little niece tells him, he thinks he knows better. "Addy K, it's gonna fall."

"I know, sweetheart."

"It won't fall..." Lance says confidently, though I suspect he is trying to save face.

"It's gonna fall," Rory repeated as the blankets' weight caused the whole thing to come tumbling down, just as we said it would.

I burst out laughing while Rory surveyed the damage, hands on her hips.

Lance's brow wrinkled while he studied the pile on the floor.

"Told ya so." I couldn't stop myself from commenting.

"Technically, this should have worked."

"Me and Addy K do it." Rory squeezes between us and sorts the lightweight blankets from the heavier ones.

"We've done this too many times to count, Lance, so why don't you take a seat and watch the experts do it." I laugh and point over to the love seat.

In no time, Rory and I had the fort built using all the pillows. We even set a few of her stuffed animals inside. Sure, it was a tighter squeeze than we are used to, but it was cozy and seemed just right to me.

"I'm ready." Rory sits between Lance and me with Mr. Deputy Bear tucked under her blanket and a bowl of popcorn in her lap.

Pointing the remote at the television, I press play and the familiar castle logo appears on the screen to signal the start of the show.

"What are we watching?" Lance reaches for some popcorn.

Rory holds her finger to her lips and playfully scolds him. "Shhhh, *Peter Pan*."

I stifle a giggle when he mouths sorry.

Dropping my voice to a barely audible whisper, I let him know the rules for our living room theater. "We have to stay quiet until intermission or we might miss part of the movie." The real reason for creating this rule was to help Rory settle down. The advantage is she rarely makes it beyond the halfway point before falling to sleep.

The three of us quietly munch on popcorn while watching one of Rory's favorite movies. It felt normal. As if we've shared a family night often. I can't stop my heart from hoping it's just the first of many. So, this is what it feels like to live in the moment.

Sure enough, right after Rory's favorite part, when Peter introduces Wendy to the mermaids, she yawns and snuggles against Lance before her eyes flutter closed. He scoots away slightly, allowing Rory's head to rest on the pillow.

"Are you okay with her laying here for just a bit longer? If we move her now, she'll wake up."

"Yeah, she's fine. Let her sleep while we finish watching the movie." He repositions the blanket over Rory's bare feet. "I forgot how good these classic cartoons are."

"I think you're just a big kid at heart."

"Busted. You uncovered my secret."

"Well, it's good you like these movies because there are times they play on constant repeat in this house."

The pirate ship sails across the sky, ending the movie. I hum along with the final song. Like most Disney songs, I know them by heart.

The lyrics aren't lost on me. Bidding my cares goodbye so I can fly would be great. I am trying to do just that. Time together tonight proves that under the right circumstances and with the right man beside me, I just might be able to let my heart fly.

Carefully, I crawl out from the fort and bend to lift Rory.

"Oof. She's getting so big."

"Let me pick her up." Lance lifts my sleeping girl as if she weighs nothing and carries her down the hall to her room. He gently rocks her from side to side while I turn down the covers. He lowers Rory to the mattress without waking her and places Mr. Deputy Bear on the pillow.

Still asleep, Rory rolls over and snuggles her toy. With the glow of the nightlight, I see a wide smile stretch across her face. She must be having happy dreams.

I reach for Lance's hand and lead him out of the room, leaving the door ajar so we don't wake her.

I give him the remote. "Here, why don't you choose something for us to watch. Would you like a beer or something else to drink?"

"More iced tea would be great."

"You got it."

When I return to the living room, I find him sitting under the tent of blankets again.

"We can take the fort down now."

"Why? I haven't had this much fun in a long time. Come join me."

"You are full of surprises." I place our drinks on the coffee table within reach and climb in beside him.

"Oh, that reminds me. I almost forgot about my secret." He opens the plastic bag he brought in with the pizzas. "I have chocolate covered caramels, red vines, and gummy fish."

"I love theatre candy. I'm glad you didn't bring them out while Rory was awake, though."

"Oh, no. Is she not allowed to have candy?" Shit, I can tell he thinks he's messed up again.

"No, it's okay. She can have a little bit of candy now and then." I pull the box close to my chest. "It's me. I just don't like to share."

"Ahh, so that's how it is." His bright smile returns and lights up his face.

"Yep." I open the box of caramels and pop a few of the treats into my mouth. The instant the chocolate melts on my tongue, I let out a pleasurable moan. When I look at Lance, his face is twisted like he's in pain. "What's wrong?"

"That noise you just made makes me want to do more than just watch TV."

The candy gets stuck in my throat. My body wants Lance,

but my head says it's not the right time to take him to bed with Rory just down the hall.

"Umm, I'm not sure that's such a good idea with Rory home."

I sense his disappointment, but he doesn't pressure me.

"It's okay. Come on, let's see what's on for us to watch." He lifts a corner of the blanket covering his legs—an invitation for me to snuggle into his side. When I scoot over and lean into his body, he lowers his arm and pulls me in close.

We sit in comfortable silence while Lance channel surfs. He stops on one of those reality cop shows. "Is it really like that, or is all this made up for TV?"

"I have a friend whose agency participated in one of these shows. She said they re-enact or stage some scenes. Like when they're driving and talking to the camera or after an arrest and the officers are debriefing. She made a point to add that none of this is ever done at risk to the officers or public safety."

"I thought all of it was real."

"Most of it is but remember it's still a form of entertainment. There is a lot they won't or can't show."

"That makes sense. What else is different from real life and TV?"

"For one, we aren't always racing to a crime scene with our lights flashing and sirens blaring. Those non-emergency calls are generally boring compared to the chases, so they cut them out."

I lean forward and turn my body to face him. "I like talking and getting to know more about you and your job."

"I suppose it's about time we got down to the nitty gritty and share these details, even if we went about this a little backward."

"I agree, so continue, please. Tell me what a typical shift looks like for you?"

He shakes his head and chuckles. "First, there's no such thing as typical or normal. I've learned to expect the unexpected and never say it's a slow night because that's when everything turns to shit."

"Alright, I'll remember that. No slow nights." I pretend to check off an imaginary list. "Tell me about some of the strange things you've seen."

"Animals seem to be some of the weirdest calls we get. You remember the story I told at Paul's funeral about the skunks and psychotic goose?"

"I remember. That story made everyone smile."

"There was one time I was working by myself after midnight. I stopped a car for running a red light. It was a man in his late sixties, nothing too unusual. I noticed he was nervously petting what I thought was a sleeping dog in the passenger seat. When I shined my flashlight on his dog, I realized it was dead, and based on the smell that hit me, the poor thing had been for a long time. I returned to my squad car and radioed for an ambulance. The man was obviously having a mental crisis and needed to be seen at the hospital."

"Gosh."

"He agreed to go after I promised to care for his pet."

I could feel my eyes welling up, and right then, I realized once more what an amazing man Lance was to do the job he did.

"That was a case I was glad to stumble upon because his daughter had been trying to reach him for months and was able to have him moved into a care home that specialized in Alzheimer's patients."

"That's so sad. I don't know how you do it." The pizza in my stomach churns, imagining all the things he deals with daily.

"Yeah, looking back, I recognize how emotional this was

for his family, but when I'm in the moment, it's just part of the job."

"It's so much more than that, Lance."

"I've become desensitized to a lot of the things I see, and as sad as it was, there is a funny part to this story. The paramedic couldn't praise me enough at first for being a great guy since I offered to care for the man's dog." He was dying to laugh. "Until I told him to go check for himself."

"I bet he was horrified."

"Yep! He threw up beside the car and called me all sorts of names while stomping back to the ambulance."

I loved hearing the tales of his life as an officer, and it was good to see his smile, and one that told me being a cop meant more to him than a simple job.

"If I remember correctly, his one finger salute out the window capped off my night."

"That's funny, but tell me another story but make it a real cop story this time."

He sinks back into the pillows. "I'm not sure what you mean by real cop story. They are all real."

"I'm just trying to get a feel for what it will be like as your girlfriend. If I have a better idea of what your job is, maybe I won't worry about you as much."

"So what you're really asking is about the potential danger. Am I right?"

"Yeah, that's part of it." A chill runs up my spine when he says danger. "What about the bad stuff? When you were gone, I started looking at some websites about life with an officer. I guess I didn't realize how different it is."

"Hey, come here." He pulls me into his lap and holds me tight. I feel safe and melt to his touch. "Let's talk about this. Tell me, what is the first thing you think of when someone says they called the police?"

"That someone is in danger, or there's a crime, and you'll get shot."

"Right, and that's why you're focusing on the bad stuff. Here's the thing, we are called to solve problems. Some of those have obvious dangers, others don't."

"But you never know and that scares the crap out of me." I close my eyes and lean my head on his shoulder.

"That's perfectly normal. In fact, I need that sense of fear to keep me alert at all times." He moves me so I'm straddling his hips, looking directly into his eyes. "I can't tell you I'll never be hurt, but here's what I can promise you. The sheriff has spent a lot of money to train me. I take what I do seriously, and my intent is always to come home in one piece. I don't take unnecessary risks. I follow the example my father set of how to treat people. He told me respect given is respect received. Just because I meet a person on the worst day of their life doesn't mean they are bad. Keeping that in mind helps me deescalate many of those potentially dangerous moments and keeps me safe."

"It's a lot to deal with. Thinking about your boyfriend being shot at on the job and letting my imagination get the best of me is hard to avoid."

"I know and I won't tell you not to worry. My mom said it took her years to not be a nervous wreck when Dad was at work. You're just starting out. Maybe when you meet, you can talk with her more about how she handled it."

"I'd like that a lot. Both parts. Meeting your parents and talking to her sound great."

"Good, because they are excited to meet you and Rory."

"You told them about us already?"

"Turns out Jackson ratted us out to my mom."

"So, you're telling me I can't share secrets with Jackson because he has a big mouth?" I frown. I'd spoken with

Jackson a lot while Lance was away and assumed I could trust him.

"Don't be mad. Jackson takes confidentiality seriously, but when there is concern about personal safety, he doesn't have a choice about acting on it. I wasn't at rock bottom, but I was closer than I care to remember. I've accepted he did the right thing." He dips his chin and swallows hard. "I don't think I'd be here with you tonight if he didn't interfere and contact my parents."

His admission stuns me. My mind swirls with thoughts of Lance and how alone he must have felt. I hate that I sat back and waited instead of going to him.

He clears his throat and reaches for his iced tea on the table. I jump when he unexpectedly presses the cold glass against my arm.

"Argh, that's cold!"

"Tension breaker. It had to happen." He grins then takes a long drink. "Our conversation was becoming way too serious. I had to do something to change the mood."

"Ha ha, very funny." Lance holds me in place when I try to climb off his lap. I'm a little annoyed he's making light of the situation. "It didn't work by the way."

"What didn't work?"

"Trying to distract me from thinking about all the horrible things that can happen to you."

"Wanna bet I can make you forget about the bad stuff." His eyes grow wide and a low sexy growl rumbles in his throat.

"What? Are you going to hypnotize me or something?" My annoyance amps up, making me sarcastic and full of sass.

"Yeah, or something."

"I know what you said earlier, but I want to kiss you."

Still sitting in his lap, his fingers are firm on my hips. He is in control.

"Just a kiss?" For weeks I've replayed our last night in my bed together and how it felt to have his hands caress my body. Thinking of that time and the promise of a replay has me wanting to give in to my desires once more.

"Yep, just one kiss." His lips brush over mine lightly. The intensity of my breathing increases. Lance uses his tongue to trace a line over my collar bone and moves south to the top of my breasts.

Breathlessly I remind him, "This is more than just one kiss."

"Who said how long a kiss has to last." Lowering me gently onto my back, he hovers over me, silently asking for permission to continue.

"Why did you stop?" My body trembles with anticipation. I should be responsible and stop this, but Lance has me under his spell, making me forget why I said no in the first place.

"Call it an intermission." His head touches the top of the fort and the makeshift walls move a little. He leans over me, sliding his fingers inside the waistband of my pajamas, tugging them down my legs. "Are we still okay?"

"Don't you dare stop. But we can't make any noise." My earlier fears of Rory finding us kissing fly out the door.

Rather than wait for Lance to continue, I switch positions. My attempt at sexy turns into an epic fail. Climbing on top of him caused our expertly built fort to tumble down around us, leaving us covered in sheets and blankets.

"Are you alright?" Lance used his body to shield me from the dining chairs that tipped over.

"Yeah, it's just that I can't breathe."

"Fuck, what hurts?" His eyes are wide with concern.

"Ugh, my lungs." I stifle a giggle and cough. "It's because, umm, you're squishing me." I push his hands away and crawl out from under the blankets.

He laughs and tosses my pajama bottoms toward me, and I pull them back on. With all the noise we made, there is a slight chance Rory will sneak out of bed and make her way here soon.

With the blankets folded and everything back in its place, Lance and I decide to spend the rest of the evening getting to know each other over bowls of ice cream.

"I only have vanilla, strawberry, and butter pecan."

"Well, since there is no chocolate…" he pouts. "How about strawberry?"

"You are such a baby, but just for you, I will be sure to have chocolate for next time."

While dishing up the ice cream, Lance comes to stand behind and whispers in my ear. "Do you know how much I love hearing you say next time?" I'm wrapped in his arms again and I can't find any reason to resist. He nuzzles my neck, making me giggle. "…how lucky I am to have a next time with you and Rory."

A sudden crashing sound from the back of the house, like breaking glass and falling metal, startles me.

"What the hell was that?" I scream, immediately rushing out of the kitchen and toward Rory's room. Lance is right behind me.

Thankfully, Rory is in her bed and unharmed, sitting up, holding her beloved bear. The sound obviously woke her.

"Addy K? I heard a noise?" I rush to her side, sit on her bed, and pull her onto my lap. Looking up to Lance, I can see his expression is that of concern. Similar to what I remember that day at Leslie's.

"Stay here. I'll check the rest of the house and call for another officer on duty to meet me outside." He hurries out of the room and quickly returns to give me my cell phone.

"Addy K, I scared." I squeeze her tight and pull the blanket around both of us.

"I won't let anything happen to either of you." Lance kisses Rory on top of her head and me on my cheek. Before closing the door, he pauses and says something so soft I almost missed it.

"I love you both."

12

LANCE

Racing outside, I call Jackson while searching for the heavy-duty flashlight I keep under the bench seat in my truck. Flicking the switch on, I focus the beam of light on the area in front of the house. I don't see anything out of place, so I continue toward the backyard when Jackson answers his phone.

"Hey, Lance. Everything alright?"

"Are you on patrol right now?"

"Yeah, I'm with Javier. What's up?"

The motion detection flood lights are triggered as I walk toward the detached garage. Seconds later, I can clearly see Kellie's car has been vandalized. The driver's side window is punched inward, with glass all over the dirt. On closer inspection, I notice her windshield is also damaged. It makes me think this could be more than just an attempted car theft.

I spot other clues that tell me this crime is not a random opportunity. With the car parked behind the house, there aren't many who would take the chance of being seen walking up the driveway. They would need to escape the same way they came in and hope they don't get caught.

The metal sound must have been when something was used to dent the hood. Whoever did this was more concerned with damaging Kellie's property and leaving her some sort of message. But who? "I'm at Kellie's. Her car windows have been busted out, but something doesn't feel right."

"In what way?" Jackson asks.

"I don't think this was a random act."

"Alright, we're not too far away from her house. Wait for us to get there before you go searching."

"Yeah, I know. Her car is parked at the back of the house by the garage. I'll meet you there."

It's not an emergency, so there are no lights and sirens to announce their arrival. I see the beam of light from their flashlights sweeping across the driveway and hear the crunch of gravel as they walk back towards me.

"Lance?" Javier calls out.

"I'm over here. I was just doing a quick survey but haven't touched or moved anything."

"Where are Kellie and Rory?" Jackson asks before searching the car.

"They're safe inside."

"Why don't you go be with them and we'll clear the area?"

"Sound's good. By the way, I found an old wooden baseball bat next to the passenger side of the car. It's too big to be Rory's. I'm sure it was used to smash the windows."

"I'll bag it for evidence. Maybe we can find some prints." Javier steps carefully around the car while using his flashlight to scan the area.

"Yeah, but we all know that's unlikely. It's pretty wet out here, making it even harder to find any prints. I doubt we will be able to pull anything we can use, but it's worth a shot."

Thanks to the entertainment industry, most people think fingerprint evidence is a given in every crime scene. In reality, there are many factors involved, and even if we do get a usable print, the person needs to be in the computerized system that maintains the records to match it up.

"Go check on your girls. We'll find you when we're done looking around."

Entering the house, I walk down the hall and softly call out to Kellie so I don't frighten her.

"Kellie, it's just me."

I push open the bedroom door and see Rory has fallen back to sleep. Kellie is still kneeling beside her bed. When she looks up and meets my gaze, she races into my arms. "Lance…" Her tone is unsteady. "What was it?"

"Shh, it's okay. You're safe. Your car is another story."

"Oh, no, why?"

"The passenger side window and windshield have been smashed."

"What? Why would someone do that?"

"Well, that's what I was going to ask you. Do you have any idea about who might want to cause you problems?"

"No clue. I keep to myself, you know that."

"Let's go into the living room so we don't wake Rory."

Looking at our sleeping girl, relief washes over me. The fear I saw written on her face when she asked Kellie what made the loud noise just about killed me.

I don't want to scare her into thinking it's more than an indiscriminate crime, but training tells me whoever did this was full of anger.

"Do you think any of the friends Leslie did drugs with know where you live?"

"Umm, it's possible, but why would they suddenly show up out of the blue?"

"We can't discount anything when piecing together evidence."

A knock on the front door causes Kellie to jump.

"Relax. I'm right here with you. I'm sure it's just Jackson." I open the door and step aside, allowing Javier to enter first. "Kellie, this is Deputy Javier Valez. You might remember him from Paul's funeral."

"Good evening, Ms. Bryant." Javier dips his chin once in greeting.

"Hi, thanks for coming so quickly." Frown lines wrinkle her forehead. She flashes a forced smile that I'm sure is meant to convince me she isn't worried. I see through it because already I know her better than she thinks.

"Hi, Jackson. Can I get you guys something to drink?"

"Thanks, but that's not necessary," Jackson answers for both men.

"We just have a few questions for our report." Javier removes a small notebook from his right breast pocket. "Do you remember if you locked the side door to your garage?"

"I never lock it. I've always felt safe and never thought it was necessary."

Her answer doesn't surprise me. It's common for the public to have a false sense of security until they are the victims of a crime.

"I suggest you make a point of locking it from now on. Come morning, you'll need to check to see if anything is missing."

"There's not much out there. Just some of Rory's baby clothes and a few of Leslie's things I saved for when she's older."

"Any ideas who would do this?"

"No. I was just telling Lance I have no clue. I work from home and rarely go out. As far as I know, this neighborhood is safe. It's why we picked this area. Lots of families with young kids."

"Do you have security cameras?"

"No, I didn't think I'd need them."

Javier and Jackson ask a few more routine questions and provide Kellie with a report number for insurance purposes.

"I'm going to walk them out to their car, but I'll be right back." I have a few more questions that Kellie doesn't need to hear.

Standing beside the squad car, I ask Jackson to arrange for extra patrol in the neighborhood.

"My gut says someone targeted Kellie. If you can set that up, I'd appreciate it. I'll have cameras and an alarm system in place by the end of the day."

"I agree. Car thieves don't shatter windshields and the vehicle doors were still locked. I'll get the patrol schedule set up with dispatch right away." I'm thankful Jackson is here to take care of this for me.

"Thanks, guys. I'll check in with you tomorrow and let you know if anything was taken from the garage." I remind them to stay safe and walk back into the house.

It's after midnight, but adrenaline has me wide awake. Not Kellie, though.

She's curled up on the couch with a blanket covering her legs. I can see she is fighting to keep her eyes open.

"How ya doing?"

"I'll be okay. I know it's late and you have work tomorrow." She yawns. I don't want her worrying all night and come up with an idea I hope she'll go along with.

"You've had a lot to deal with tonight. I agree it's not time for us to share a bed, but I need to know you and Rory are safe. How about you go to your bedroom and I sleep on the couch?"

"I can't ask you to do that."

"You didn't, I offered."

She tries to hide another yawn. "Okay, I'm too tired and don't want to fight you on this. Plus, having you here will make me feel better."

Reaching for her hand, I help her to her feet and pull her in for a hug to settle my own nerves. When she melts into me, I feel some of the tension in my muscles relax.

I kiss her cheek. “Get some rest, sweetheart.”

“Good night, Sir Lancelot. Thanks for saving us again.”

“I promise to always be here to protect both of you.”

It’s been a week with no further incidents. In fact, no reports of any problems in the surrounding area either. If a car thief was making their rounds, there would be other related crimes, but nothing stands out.

Thankfully, Kellie isn’t as jumpy when she hears a noise from outside. I want her to feel safe in her own home. She even allowed me to have a full security system installed with twenty-four-hour monitoring. It’s helped put both of our minds at ease.

It doesn’t mean I’ve stopped investigating. I did a little digging and found more information about Rory’s father. I knew he was killed shortly after we found him passed out in Leslie’s apartment. Turns out he was an only child and his parents died when he was a teen. No surprise, they were addicted to drugs and died in a fire at a house used to cook meth. Stephen lived with his grandmother, who died a few years ago from a heart attack at seventy-eight. With no relatives to be found alive, I’ve ruled out the possibility that he is somehow connected to the crime.

I’ve been swamped with paperwork for tomorrow's academy graduation and have been asked to speak at the commencement ceremony. Kellie has agreed to attend the graduation and the celebration that follows.

My phone rings and Kellie’s picture appears on my screen.

"Hello, gorgeous. I was just thinking about you."

"You always say that."

"Because it's true."

"Anyway." I can picture her rolling her eyes and grin to myself. "I want to firm up our plans for tomorrow. Am I still meeting you there?"

"Yeah, it's easiest since I have to be there early." As one of the training instructors, I'm expected to help with the pre-graduation formalities. There are also a few traditions to welcome the rookies into the Springhill Sheriff's Department. The recruit's final assignment is an early morning, five-mile run. The town gathers on Main Street to support the new officers and concludes with a pancake breakfast to raise money for charity.

"Sounds good. My parents are keeping Rory for the weekend, so we won't have to rush home."

"I'm excited to show you off at your first family meeting at Heath's at the after party."

She clears her throat. "I thought if you wanted to bring an overnight bag, umm, since Rory won't be home…" Her voice trails off. I can tell she's nervous. The last thing I want is for her to feel pressured to have sex again before she's ready and I certainly don't want her to think of my hesitation as rejection, so I try to soften my response.

"Tell you what. I always have my go bag ready. When you feel the time is right, you just give me a sign. Maybe we can work out a code. For instance, you can say purple unicorns, and I'll know that means it's go time." I hold my breath and wait to hear her reaction. Relief washes over me when I hear her burst out with laughter.

"And here I thought you'd jump at the chance to spend the night with me again." She sounds more relaxed.

As glad as I am that my silly attempt to lighten the mood worked, I need her to know how much I really do want her.

"Oh, Kellie, don't get me wrong. I am ready and more than willing, but before we take that huge leap again, we need to be 100% positive it's the right time because as soon as we do, there will be no turning back."

"You're right. Thanks for being the levelheaded one in this relationship. At least you chose a code I won't forget. Shit, my boss is calling. I'll see you tomorrow."

"I can't wait. See you then." I disconnect the call and feel a smile stretch across my face.

Great, now I'll be thinking about stupid purple unicorns for the rest of the day.

~

The graduation starts in just a few minutes. Kellie is supposed to text me when she arrives, but I haven't heard from her.

Lance: Are you here yet?

When she doesn't answer right away, I scroll through my old text messages, deleting the ones I don't need to save. I stop when I get to Patricia's last message, sent just after her uninvited visit to my house. I made sure to keep it just in case I needed evidence of her stalking. She apologized and wished me luck with my new relationship. Her sudden change from stalker to pleasant and supportive has me wondering if this isn't just the calm before the storm.

My phone vibrates.

. . .

Kellie: Yeah, I just got here. Sorry, I didn't think parking would be so bad. Jackson helped me find my seat.

Lance: Shit. I should have told you to park around back by my truck.

Kellie: It's fine. I'm just glad I changed from my four-inch heels to the comfortable flats.

Lance: Now I'm extra sorry I forgot about the parking. Any chance I can get you to wear those sexy shoes tonight?

Kellie: I'll think about it. LOL

Lance: I need to get lined up to walk on stage. Thanks for helping with my speech last night.

Kellie: You're welcome, and don't worry, you'll be great. xoxo

I slide my phone into the inside pocket of my coat. Standing beside my fellow instructors, we wait for the signal to begin marching down the aisle. The last time I wore this dress uniform was at Paul's funeral with Kellie beside me. She might not be standing on stage with me, but I made sure I could see her clearly from where I was seated because I need her support again.

I lower my head and place my hand over my racing heart.

Under my palm, I feel the outline of Paul's patch that I stitched under the lining last night. Technically, by sewing it to my uniform, I'm breaking our dress code, but I need something from my partner to get me through my speech.

My turn to address the class came quicker than I'd anticipated. I knew the lineup, but I was distracted watching Kellie in the audience and almost missed my introduction. Walking to the podium, I see her smiling brightly, and my earlier nerves disappear.

"I want to thank Sheriff Roberts for allowing me to participate in today's graduation for the 119th academy class. Each speaker has a different message to share." I pause for breath. "While mine may not be what you expect from a celebration such as this, I feel it's essential and a life lesson I hope you'll carry with you throughout your time as a law enforcement officer."

Scanning the crowded room of fellow officers, their families, and friends, my hope is that more than just the class will benefit from my speech.

"The time spent teaching at the academy has been one of the highlights of my career. Watching these recruits grow and support each other while reaching their goals through hard work, determination, and sacrifice was inspiring. Their enthusiasm reminded me why I chose this career."

Breathing in deeply, I find Kellie in the crowd and see the pride in her eyes.

"Along with your training, you have formed an unbreakable bond with your classmates. You will rely on them to keep you safe. You will celebrate the good times and comfort them through the sad, but the important part is, you will be there for one another."

My hands begin to shake. I turn over the paper I was reading from and decide to speak from my heart instead.

"I met my best friend, Deputy Paul Lancaster, during our

academy class seven years ago. I can vividly remember standing next to him after our graduation. We couldn't wait to wear our new crisp blue uniform, strap a duty belt around our waist, a gun to our hip and walk into the world to protect the community. We thought we were invincible."

I pause and look out into the sea of faces, trying to gauge their reactions.

"Unfortunately, Paul can't be with us today because no one is invincible. My best friend took his life on June 10th of this year."

And there it is. The smiles have disappeared, replaced with a look of shock and sadness.

"It has taken me many sleepless nights to piece together the puzzle of why he decided to kill himself, and though I will never fully understand his decision, I can try to use his death to hopefully save lives."

I look at Kellie again. This time I see her dabbing at her eyes with a handkerchief. The same one I gave her the day we met, and she used it to wipe away her tears while watching her sister overdose.

"I never intended to speak so openly about Paul's suicide, but I've come to realize if I remain silent, we may lose more officers." I leave my words with the audience for a few seconds, knowing how imperative it is that they sink in. "Preventing law enforcement suicide is essential and providing services without stigma for those seeking assistance must become a priority for police agencies nationwide." I turn to Jackson who nods his approval. "Whether you want to believe it or not, being a first responder will take a toll on your mental health."

My chest tightens and I hold my breath to stay in control. Just when I thought the pain would overcome me, a voice from the crowd calls out, "We're here for you, Deputy Malloy." Another shouts, "You got this, Lance."

I close my eyes and take a deep breath to suppress my emotions. When I open them, I see my work family watching and giving me the strength to continue. Lieutenant Cartwright stands and offers me a glass of water. After sipping some of the cool liquid, I place it on the shelf under the podium.

"During your career as an officer, you will witness the worst in humanity—senseless loss of lives, unprovoked violence, and hatred that cannot be explained. There will be images from traumatic events you won't be able to erase from your mind. You might convince yourself that it is just part of the job and not give it another conscious thought, but it's still there. When not in uniform, everyday life stresses may pile up and weigh on you because you're not a robot. You are human and, as such, allowed to have emotions just like everyone else in this world."

A few of the veteran officers nod their agreement.

"I implore you to put your mental health first. Don't wait until you hit rock bottom as Paul did before reaching out to your family. Please remember, admitting you need help is not a sign of weakness. It requires courage to acknowledge your feelings and say you can't do it alone."

I turn to Jackson again and the full impact of how he saved my life hits me. "Our peer support is run by some of the best men and women I know. They don't judge and are only a phone call away." I keep eye contact with Jackson while I continue. "I know this to be true because I've made that call myself."

Placing my right hand over my heart, I imagine a time when Paul was alive. I can almost see him wearing his patch and take strength from the good times we shared.

"I know I've focused on the difficult parts of our job, but being a law enforcement officer is rewarding too. There are many times you will see the best in humankind. You will make a positive difference in more lives than you can count and that's why we do it. It's because of those people, we put our lives on the line."

I look at the assembled crowd and pray my words have made a difference to at least one person listening today.

"Thank you for the opportunity to share Paul's story as well as my own. My hope is that his death wasn't in vain but a reminder that your family of blue is always here and will support you. Congratulations again to the 119th academy class. Welcome to the Springhill Sheriff's Department. And never forget, from this moment on, no matter where you go in life, you will always be forever blue."

13

KELLIE

"You did fantastic, Lance. I'm so proud of you." We meet halfway across the room. I wrap my arms around his neck and hold on tight while he lifts me into a hug.

"I'm not so sure. It wasn't anything like I practiced last night."

"It made me feel sad, but your words were lovely."

"I guess I got lost in the emotions and felt my message would be better received if they just heard me talk."

Lance kisses my cheek and lowers me to my feet.

"It was perfect. I heard some of the recruits and their families discussing how much they appreciated what you said. I know talking about Paul wasn't easy but sharing that little bit of yourself had to be even harder."

"I guess you're right." He takes my hand and leads us outside. "Come on, I'll walk you to your car."

I stop to look at him. "You know, when you admitted you accepted help, you put a face to it. That took courage."

He looks down at his feet. He doesn't want to hear the praise I'm bestowing upon him because he doesn't believe he deserves it. I know differently because today, he put his heart out for the world to see, perhaps one of the bravest things he will ever do.

"The Sheriff asked me if I would consider speaking at future ceremonies. He thinks my story and experiences are something all recruits should hear. Maybe even do a class at the academy and include the families, so they understand the part they play in the life of an officer."

I feel so proud of him. "What did you tell him?"

"I said I would need to think on it because as much as I want to help, it's not easy talking about Paul's death."

"In time, it will get easier."

"Yeah, and maybe it won't hurt so much, but right now, it still feels too raw." His voice cracks. "I almost lost it at one point while speaking and I'm not so sure I can do it again."

"I saw you stumble, and I also heard and saw your fellow officers support you."

"They weren't the only ones keeping me going. Looking out and seeing you helped me more than you know." He brings my hand up to his lips and gently kisses my knuckles. "You give me strength."

"I could say the same about you. Guess we are a pretty good team."

"A great team." We walk a little further away from the crowd. "I plan to schedule a meeting with Sheriff Roberts next month before the new academy class starts. By then, I should have an answer."

"Did he know you were planning on talking about Paul?"

"Yes, I ran it by him, and he approved the outline but didn't know the exact details."

"Then he obviously felt the subject was appropriate."

"Excuse me, Instructor Malloy, may I have a moment of your time?" One of the new officers approaches us. He looks very young, but I'm assuming he's only a few years younger than me. Beside him is a stunning woman holding a newborn baby swaddled in a pink blanket.

"It's no longer Instructor Malloy. We are both deputies now, so please call me Lance." The men shake hands.

"Yes, sir. It will be hard to get used to that." The baby coos and reminds me of Rory when she was that small. "I'd like you to meet my family. This is my wife, Chelsea, and my daughter, Serena."

"Nice to meet you, Mrs. Timmons. You have a beautiful daughter." Lance links our fingers again. "This is my girlfriend, Kellie."

My heart picks up the pace when he introduces me as his girlfriend. "Congratulations on your graduation and new baby. It's wonderful to meet all three of you."

"Thank you. It's been a busy month with Frank's final exams and Serena coming a month early, but we couldn't be happier." Chelsea looks at her husband with so much love it makes me realize how much I want the same from Lance.

"Instructor Malloy, um, I mean Lance, I want to thank you for all you did for our class." He fidgets with his hat in his hands. "Also, you should know your speech today hit close to home for me."

"It did?" Lance asks.

"Yes, Sir. My brother killed himself when he was sixteen, and I know you were talking about law enforcement, but nobody is immune to suffering from mental health problems. I want you to know I heard you loud and clear. Thank you for having the courage to lead us by example."

"I'm deeply sorry about your brother. Don't forget, if you ever need anything, please do not hesitate to call me."

"Yes, sir, I'll remember that." The baby fusses, and Deputy Timmons takes her from Chelsea's arms, cuddling her close to his chest.

Holy hell, my biological alarm clock just went off. Is there anything more magical than a daddy looking into the eyes of his child?

Yes, there is, and it's right in front of me. Put that daddy in a sexy as sin uniform and my hormones have shifted into overdrive. I'm a little stunned by my reaction. It's like mother nature just took over my body.

Sure, I've always thought about having my own child but never experienced this rush of emotions. I've never felt such a strong desire as this to have a baby.

"Are you coming to Heath's to celebrate?" Lance asks, distracting me from the unexplained baby fever currently occupying my thoughts.

"No, I'll be taking my little family home and having a quiet night. I have a feeling I won't have a lot of free nights in my future. Gotta take advantage of them when I can."

"That you do. Have a great night and I'll see you at the station soon."

Watching the couple walk away tugs at my heartstrings. I can almost picture Lance holding a newborn baby and wonder if that's something he would even want. Rory occupies so much of my time already. How time consuming would it be to have two children that depended on me? With the current images running through my mind, I better have this monumental discussion with Lance soon.

Before we can get much further, we are stopped again.

"Lance, wait up," Jackson calls out. "Are you leaving already?"

"Just taking Kellie to her car. I need to stay for a little longer. What's up?" Jackson falls in step with us as we continue walking to the parking area.

"I want you to know how proud I am of what you did today. I know it couldn't be easy to talk about Paul so soon, but your selfless act today will save lives."

"That's all I can hope for and to keep Paul's memory

alive." Lance swallows hard. I've learned to read his nonverbal cues very well and I can tell he needs to change the subject.

"How much longer do you have before you can leave? I may take a nap. I don't get to stay out late very often." This was meant to lighten the mood, but after waking up early with Rory this morning, re-charging my batteries sounds like an excellent plan. Maybe it will keep me from dozing off at 9 pm.

"Probably another hour or so. We still need to take the group picture, and often the deputies and their families want individual pictures with the instructors."

"Okay, I'll take off then and meet you later at Heath's."

"Hey, Malloy. You need to get over here for the picture." The man I recognize as Lieutenant Cartwright is waving Lance over to the group setting up in front of the building.

"Shit, Jackson, would you mind walking Kellie to her car?"

"Are you kidding? The chance to have this beautiful woman on my arm. Of course, I'll take your place." A blush warms my cheeks.

"Watch it, Deputy Locke."

Jackson laughs and pats Lance's shoulder. "You're so easy to razz. Go do what you need to do, and I'll get Kellie safely to her car."

Lance pulls me in for a kiss that is just a little too sexy for public view, but I can't find it in me to stop him.

"Ahem," Jackson clears his throat. "Ah, I hate to be the bad guy, Lance, but they are waiting on you."

Another light brush of his lips over mine and our kiss ends, leaving me breathless. He whispers in my ear so Jackson doesn't hear. "Don't forget to wear those sexy high heels you promised."

My heart thuds against my chest and the butterflies in my

belly dance with delight as I watch my gorgeous deputy saunter off to join the others.

"Hey, Lance!" He stops and turns on his heel to face me.

"Yeah? What's wrong?"

"Nothing, just eh, I wanted to say..." Without reservations, I holler, "Purple Unicorn!"

~

"Addy K, I made s'ghetti with Grumpa!" Rory's excited voice bellows through my car speakers while driving to Heath's. Because I am not there, my gorgeous niece thinks she has to shout. I meant to call her earlier but really did take a nap and now I'm running behind.

"Hi, kiddo. That's fantastic. You'll have to teach me so we can have it at home sometime soon."

"That's what Gram Gram said."

"Did she now?"

"She said I should make it for you and Lance like in *Lady and the Tramp*."

"Rory has big plans to make a special dinner for you two." Mom chuckles in the background. "She even asked how to make one long noodle so you can kiss."

"I'll have to run that one past him tonight." As I suspected, Rory has fallen head over heels in love with Lance.

I finally told my parents about dating Lance after the car incident. They were grateful he was at the house when it happened.

Mom in particular was thrilled to hear I was dating. Dad pulled the protective father routine, telling me how he wants to meet the young man who will be around his girls. It was all an act because I could see him fighting back a smile. I know he is happy for me, but when they talk, I suspect it will be the cliché, what are your intentions with my daughter conversation.

"I gotta go. I'm pulling into the parking lot. I'll call you tomorrow. Have fun making spaghetti. Love you lots."

"Bye Addy K, love you more."

I press the button to disconnect the call. Not finding any parking in the front lot, I circle around and drive to the back. Finally, a spot opens, and it happens to be near Lance's truck. I'm glad he's here already.

Entering the bar, it's wall to wall cops. I expected everyone to be wearing their dress uniform, but most have changed into casual clothes. Now I'm glad I put on a less formal dress, but I still needed something to go with the heels Lance requested I wear, just for him. I can't wait to see his expression when he looks at me in this new, fitted, red mini-dress.

I see Lance leaning against the bar, talking animatedly with his friends. Slowly, I sneak up behind him, stand on tiptoes pressing my lips close to his ear, and whisper.

"Hi, Deputy. How 'bout you buy me a drink?"

"I'm sorry, ma'am, I'm waiting for the most beautiful girl in the world to join me." He spins me around and kisses me passionately before I can respond.

"Wow." I blink a few times to regain my focus. "That was unexpected."

"You can always expect kisses, babe." He playfully rubs his nose against mine while looking into my eyes.

"What do you want to drink?"

"I'm driving, remember. Just tea tonight."

"Tea?"

"I know, I'm such a boring date, but since I'm dating a cop, he wouldn't like me breaking the law." I shoot a wink his way.

He returns my flirting with a dazzling smile, melting me.

Could he be any sexier? "Not boring, little lady but responsible, I approve." Lance signals the bartender and orders my tea. He adds a large basket of French fries to the order with a side of mustard, mayo, and ketchup. It's so cute how he remembers the little things.

"Aww, it's just like the first time we saw each other."

"No, sweetheart, you're wrong." He looks at me with longing. I see the desire in his eyes, the gentle biting of his bottom lip, and the way he tilts his head to the side. "The first time was at that horrible apartment when I fell in love with the strong woman caring for her family. The second time was here at Heath's at the bachelorette party. That's when I realized my love for you was true."

Lance has introduced me to so many people I've lost track of all their names. After getting our drinks, Jackson found us a table to share. I'm glad because although these heels are sexy, they are killing me already.

"Of course, we play pranks on the rookies. It's a rite of passage." Seeing him laugh and joke with his co-workers has shown me a different side of him. Even the first night at Heath's, he wasn't this much fun. His smiles are genuine, showing off the dimple that's been hiding behind his guarded façade.

I'm sitting in a booth between Jackson and Lance. Across from us are Javier, Joe, and Bennett. I think those are their names. I've sat quietly just listening to the conversation, but this subject caught my attention.

"What kind of pranks?"

"Just stupid stuff," Javier says. "Like tell the rookie to call in to dispatch and ask for rubber cuffs used for suspects who are allergic to metal."

"I don't understand. Why is that a prank?"

"Because there's no such thing as rubber handcuffs." Lance chuckles and tugs me into his side. "See, it's just a stupid joke that doesn't even make sense to anyone, yet we still do it."

"Did they get you with any of their tricks?"

Lance shakes his head. "Jackson tried several times but never got me. I grew up listening to my dad and his friends talk about the shenanigans cops pulled. I was prepared and ruined their plans each time they tried."

"After a year, I finally gave up." Jackson takes a drink from his beer, finishing it. "I need another one. This round is on me."

With Jackson at the bar, I'm no longer wedged in and use this opportunity to run to the bathroom. I whisper to Lance, "I need to use the restroom. Be right back." Miracles do happen. There was no line. Maybe that's because there must be ten men to every one woman tonight.

Washing my hands, the fine hairs on the back of my neck prickle me. I'm bumped out of the way when someone reaches for a towel from the dispenser.

"Excuse me." I know that voice and my stomach churns. "Oh, hi, Kellie. I didn't know that was you."

I look up in the mirror and see the evilest person I know standing behind me. Her devilish smile makes me shudder. "Trish. Hi."

"Well, don't you look cute in your little thrift store dress." She looks me up and down. "I'm sure as a single mom, you don't get out often enough to buy anything new. Am I right?" She removes a tube of lip gloss from her purse and swipes it over her lips.

"Uh…um…" Stunned by her blatant rudeness, I can't think of a comeback to save my life.

"It's okay, Kellie. I understand completely. I wonder if

your boyfriend likes what you're wearing." With a hand on her hip, she cocks an eyebrow and snorts. "No, I didn't think so, either."

She turns on her heels and exits the bathroom leaving me standing, open mouthed and completely dumbstruck. I can't understand how one woman can be so wicked or what I could have done to be the subject of this recent attack.

I'm angry and focus on slowing my breathing. It only takes a few minutes for me to regain my composure. I use a wet towel to pat my face, allowing the water to cool my heated cheeks and help calm my nerves.

Looking at my reflection in the mirror, I give myself a pep talk.

"Don't let that bitch ruin your night."

Pushing the door open, I'm surprised to see Jackson leaning against the wall just a few steps away.

"You know the men's room is over there, right?" I point to the opposite side of the room.

"Yeah, I know. Lance asked me to walk you back to our booth."

I scrunch up my face, confused as to why he sent Jackson to wait for me. "It's not that far away. Did he think I'd get lost?"

"Come on." His avoidance of my question has me worried.

We make our way through the maze of tables and people standing around in groups talking. When I turn the corner to our booth, I freeze, causing Jackson to bump into me from behind. "What the fuck is she doing? And why is she touching Lance?"

I blink a few times, hoping what I see in front of me isn't real. Trish and Lance are standing beside our table, talking. Seeing her reach out and cup Lance's cheek has the internal rage I pushed down a moment ago ready to explode. It's obvious they know one another.

Turning to leave, Jackson blocks my escape. "Wait, it's not what you think."

"Oh, yeah, well tell me. What exactly am I thinking?" With my hands on my hips, I glare at him. "Maybe that you were sent to keep me away while Lance was doing whatever he's doing with her?"

"Actually, yes, he did. But not for the reason you think."

"Again, Mr. Mindreader..." I snap sarcastically "...use your powers to enlighten me on what you think I know." I don't care if I sound like a raging bitch because, at this moment, that's precisely what I am.

"Please slow down and let Lance explain."

"Why should I do that?" Arms crossed over my chest, I try to look tough when in truth, I'm dying inside.

"You need to take another look." Jackson gently places his hands on my shoulders to turn me around.

The scene has changed and so has Lance's posture. Tight jaw, stiff shoulders, and I can see his nostrils flare on each exhale of breath.

Trish's eyes are wide. Her arms crossed over her belly. When she reaches for Lance's hand, he pulls away before she can touch him. Lance says something in a low growl I see but cannot hear and shakes his head slowly. She opens her mouth to speak, but he puts up a hand to cut her off.

"Stop! Don't say another word!" His change in tone has drawn everyone's attention. "Stay the fuck away from me. And, if you come anywhere near Kellie or Rory, I won't wait for someone else to deal with you. Do you understand me now?"

Trish shudders and her eyes dart around to the crowd watching the performance.

As if the disturbance has never happened, Trish schools

her expression. Her glower turns to innocence with a painted-on smile. The spoiled brat attitude she just displayed is now calm and under control. "Yes, Deputy Malloy. I heard everything you said."

"Good."

Trish turns away from Lance but only takes two steps before looking in my direction. My skin crawls as her eyes lock onto mine. I refuse to back down and glare back at her just as intensely, hoping she can't see my fear.

Our stare down lasts long enough for her to give me a glimpse of the devil living inside her mind. I swallow hard, barely breaking eye contact. I want to blink but don't. Suddenly, she lets out a false but maniacal laugh. She must think she's won some sort of contest, only I wasn't playing.

With a little wave in my direction and the confidence of a runway model, she struts toward the front door. As she leaves, she turns one last time and flashes a smile my way. This woman is a psycho. I'd be just as crazy as her to underestimate her and what she might be capable of.

14

LANCE

"Fucking bitch," I snarl through gritted teeth. Anger courses through my body and threatens to boil over when Patricia's comments replay in my mind.

"But Lance. I wuv you." Remembering the cutesy baby voice she used when talking to me makes my stomach churn.

"For the last time. I don't love you. In fact, now that I know what love feels like, I realize I never loved you at all."

"But how can you want Kellie instead of me? She's nothing but a worn out, used up, single mom to a snot-nosed brat her drug addicted mother couldn't even love."

That's when I lost it. It's one thing for her to annoy me but insulting Kellie and the vile things she said about Rory had me ready to explode. Now I see Patricia for what she is; a cold hearted, ruthless excuse for a woman who will do anything to get what she wants.

Rage like I've never known threatens to overwhelm me but lashing out at a woman isn't in my nature, and aside from that, my training forces me to take a step back before I consider doing something I would regret. Truth is, I wanted to slap her hand away when she touched my cheek, but knowing her like I do, she'd twist it into more which would have caused even bigger problems.

A hand on my shoulder has me spinning around, ready to fight. "Don't fucking touch me!" The guttural sound from my throat is unfamiliar.

"Whoa, Lance. Calm down." Jackson puts his hands up and takes a step back. "Javier is following Patricia and will make sure she leaves without causing more trouble."

"Good." I squeeze my eyes tight shut. Rubbing my forehead, I take a few cleansing breaths to clear my mind. "Wait, I told you to stay with Kellie. Where is she?" The minute I saw Patricia walk into the bar, I asked Jackson to go find her.

"She was pretty shaken up after she saw you with Patricia. I took her into the game room to settle her nerves and asked the new waitress to sit with her until I came back."

"I need to see her now." Before I can walk away, Jackson stops me.

"Not yet. You need to get yourself under control before you go storming back in there."

"Shit." My fists clench and unclench. With each tight squeeze, I feel my knuckles crack. "Just how much did she see?"

"Enough to confuse her. She wants to know how you know Patricia."

"What did you tell her?"

"That you'd explain once you've calmed down."

"Alright." He steps to the side, blocking me again. "What now?"

"I'm not going to let you fuck this up. You need to pull yourself together. If you try talking to her with this much anger inside you, it won't go well." He hands me a glass of iced water. "Drink."

I've come to depend on him and listen to his words

without a second thought. The cool liquid works to slow the vibrations manifested from my rising temper.

"There, are you happy?" A woman from the table nearby gasps when I place the empty glass on the table harder than I intended. "Now, if you don't mind, I'd like to go find my girlfriend."

"I do mind. Listen to me, just for one moment."

"I need to sort it with Kellie."

"Then think on this; not only did Kellie just see you with another woman who she'll find out is your ex-girlfriend, but she also saw you go full-on cop mode for the first time. You forget how intimidating our demeanor is when that happens."

"What did you expect me to do? If you heard the things she said about Kellie and Rory, you would have acted the same way."

My head throbs like I've been kicked with a steel toe boot. I sway on the spot then grasp the back of the bench seat to steady myself.

"Why don't you sit down before you fall over. I'll check on Kellie." Jackson helps guide me into the booth.

"That's probably a good idea." I lean my head back and close my eyes to stop the room from spinning. I'm sure this is just the same kind of adrenaline drop I've experienced after having to chase a suspect or after arriving on the scene of an active crime.

"Alright, man. Stay here and I'll bring her to you." He places a full beer bottle in front of me and walks towards the game room.

The beer is warm, but I drink it anyway. It can't be a coincidence that Patricia showed up tonight. I knew she was too calm and quiet after her last text. I'll bet she's been planning this confrontation for weeks. Waiting for the perfect time to pounce.

Tipping the bottle back, I drain it and reach for another. I need to come up with a way to explain what just happened and hope my reaction didn't scare Kellie away.

~

"Lance." Kellie approaches cautiously as if I were an injured animal and I suppose in some ways I am. My snarled threat to leave Kellie and Rory alone was not issued lightly.

She slides into the seat across from me and takes my hand in hers. The scent of her light floral perfume centers me, and with each inhaled breath, my muscles relax.

We sit in silence for several minutes. I can feel her gentle touch giving me the strength I need to keep me in my seat. Just having her near has the pounding in my head easing.

"I'm so sorry. I didn't ever want you to see me like that." I don't look up because I'm terrified I'll see disgust reflecting back at me through her eyes.

"Do you mean I should have never seen you with Trish?"

"Partially, but mainly because I didn't want you to see me lose my temper."

"We all lose our temper, Lance."

"Yeah, I know, but I never display anger like that." Huffing out an exasperated breath, I open my eyes. Kellie's lips are pursed, eyes rimmed red, and tears have stained her cheeks.

"You might not want to talk about it, but before we go any farther, I need to know how you know Trish." She bites her lip, and I can see she's fighting back more tears.

"I'm sorry. I should have told you sooner. Remember when I mentioned the girl I used to date that hated my job?" She nods. "Well, she's my crazy ex-girlfriend."

"Hold on." She releases my hand and I miss the connection immediately. "Gina's cousin, Trish, is your ex? Well, that explains a lot. But why didn't you tell me the night of the bachelorette party?"

"I swear, I had no idea she was related to your friend Gina. I never met any of her family. We broke up the night I was supposed to meet her dad and stepmom at their anniversary party." I rub the back of my neck. My body temperature has dropped, and I feel clammy.

"That doesn't explain why you didn't mention it when I came over to apologize for her taping the paper cock onto your zipper."

"Patricia and I have been broken up for a long time. When I saw you at the bachelorette party, it didn't seem like the right time to tell you she was my ex." She uses the back of her wrist to wipe away a tear sliding down her cheek. My lack of communication has hurt her again. "I know it was a mistake, and if I could go back, I'd tell you right away."

Kellie picks at the label from my empty bottle of beer. Her brow is wrinkled as she concentrates on her task, or more likely, she's sorting through everything that has happened. Bits of paper make a small pile on the table, but she doesn't stop until each scrap has been removed. When she sits back and huffs out a deep breath, I hold perfectly still and wait for her reaction.

"Unfortunately, it's not my first run in with her."

"What do you mean?"

"I've been the target of her snide remarks and rudeness since Gina's party."

"I'm sorry you've had to deal with her."

"I can handle most things, but it all makes sense now."

"What does?" I was supposed to be the cop, but I wasn't connecting the dots to what she was trying to say.

"At Gina's family functions, Trish seems to find me, and even tonight, she surprised me in the bathroom, running her mouth like usual. I just assumed she was a raging bitch to everyone."

Through gritted teeth, I ask, "What did she say to you in there?"

"Just something stupid about my dress and asked if my boyfriend approved." Kellie pulls on the sleeve of her dress then places her hands in her lap.

"For the record, I very much approve of every part of you, no matter what you wear. You know, she's just jealous of how hot you look." She chuckles softly, but I can tell she's still upset. "Please don't be angry. I wasn't trying to keep anything from you."

"I know that now, but when I saw her touch you, I wanted to run away."

"What stopped you?"

"Jackson told me to look again." Her gaze shifts to where Trish and I were standing earlier. "You didn't like her touching you."

"No, I didn't." Reaching across the table, I gently turn her head so I can look into her eyes. "Your touch is the only one I want."

I need to be closer and move to sit on the bench beside her. Not caring who might be watching, I lean in and lightly press my lips to hers. It only takes a few seconds for me to want more. What started out as a chaste, tender kiss became sensual and demanding.

The lights in the bar are dimmed enough for us to share this private moment, but I don't care who sees me kiss my girlfriend.

"Your lips are the only ones I want." I nip her bottom lip and whisper, "You are my everything."

"Lance." Her sultry tone washes over me.

My intention was to steal a kiss but has unexpectedly switched to a feverish pace, no doubt from the built-up passion we've both held at bay. She parts her lips on a soft moan, and I dip my tongue inside for just a small sample of what Kellie has to offer. When her hands begin to wander, I realize she has other plans.

"Fuck." I groan with pleasure as her fingers brush over my cock.

Pausing to catch our breath, I see Kellie's cheeks are flushed, and the sparkle is back in her eyes.

"Hey, Lance?" She flashes a mischievous smile. "I have a great idea."

"And what would that be?" I swallow hard and shift in my seat, hoping to alleviate some of the pressure behind my zipper.

"How about you take me home so we can talk about mystical animals?"

"What?" Kellie must have short circuited my brain because I have no idea what she's talking about.

She chews on her bottom lip, barely able to keep from giggling. "You know the ones. The mystical purple unicorns."

"If you don't get that door open soon, your neighbors are going to get one hell of a show." Now that Kellie has given me the green light, or in this case, purple, I don't want to waste another minute. Pulling her back against my chest, my hands skim over the outside of her dress and palm her breasts.

"You're not making this easy, you know." She moans softly and misses fitting the key into the lock again. "If you'd stop distracting me, I might be able to see straight and get us inside."

"You don't really want me to stop," I whisper in her ear. Brushing her hair back, I sink my teeth into her neck, hoping to hit that balance between pleasure and pain. "Do you?"

She tips her head to the side and leans back against my chest. "You're right and if you stop, I may kill you." I take the key from her hand and turn the lock, opening the door and pushing it too hard. It makes a loud banging sound as it hits the wall.

We barely make it inside before we are clawing at each other's clothes. While she pulls at my shirt, I reach behind her back to unzip the dress. We fumble, getting tangled up in our desire to get naked as fast as possible.

"This isn't working very well." She drops her hands and gives up trying to pull my shirt off.

"Let's try this another way. Stand still." She does as I ask. I walk in a slow circle around her while I take in her beauty from all angles. I pause to trace my fingers down her spine causing a visible shiver to run up her body. When I stand in front of her, again she reaches out for me, but I step back, just out of reach. "No touching."

"Well, that's hardly fair." Kellie pushes out her bottom lip and pretends to pout.

"You'll have your turn shortly. For now, I want to play." I slowly slide my hands under her dress, my fingertips caressing her silky skin until I find the lace of her panties. Meeting her gaze, I smirk then hook my fingers on each side, tearing the lingerie from her body. "Let's get rid of these."

"Hey! What if those were my favorite?" Her hands rest on her hips as if she's angry. I see right through her pursed lips and wrinkled brow to the smile she's struggling to keep from showing.

This playful back and forth before sex is something I've never shared with another woman. This isn't the frenzied lust we shared on our first night together. Nor is it the sensual, slow lovemaking from the following morning where we took our time and explored each other's bodies. What we have right now is fun and must be what true love is like. Kellie is the first woman I've ever loved, and if things go as planned, she will be the only woman to ever hold my heart.

"Be honest with me. Were they really your favorite?" I have zero regrets for tearing the lace from her body. I'll take her shopping for more sexy lingerie to replace these and have spares for next time.

"No, I was just asking what if," she coos. "You may continue now." Her smartass remark makes me laugh.

"Oh, I see," I chuckle and decide to play along. "You're going to play Ms. Sassy pants tonight, is that it?" I sweep her off her feet and throw her over my shoulder.

"Put me down, silly."

"Nope, sorry, can't do that." I am smiling, but she can't see it. I march down the hall.

"You're going to pay when I get down from here."

"Is that so?" I slap her behind and she lets out a stream of girlish giggles.

"Yes, put me down, right this minute." She squeals and swats at my backside but can't quite reach. For a moment, I imagine this is the tone she uses to scold Rory for bad behavior.

"No, ma'am. We do this my way tonight." I gently lower her onto the mattress.

She rests on her elbows. Her eyes find mine. "And what exactly is your way?"

"My plan…" I move to kneel between her thighs, "…is to see how many times I can make you beg."

She shoots me that *I dare you* look then rolls her eyes before she flops back, resting her head on the pillows. "I never beg, so I guess tonight is a total bust."

"Challenge accepted." Sliding the skirt part of her dress up, my lips brush over her bare skin. Playing the game is intoxicating. She knows what she's doing to me, but I say nothing because my actions must speak louder than my words.

"Well…?" With an arched eyebrow, she teases me, forcing my hand.

"Good things come to those who wait."

"You know how much I want you, Lance."

"And I want you too, all of you."

She closes her eyes as I control the moment. Slipping a finger inside her, her hips move slowly, and without words, her body tells me she wants more. Another finger and almost instantly, I regret issuing my challenge since my throbbing cock is the one doing all the begging right now.

Slowly, I use my fingers to massage the walls of her vagina.

I lick my lips, impatient for my chance to slide my cock into her. Pulling my fingers out, I lean in and bury my tongue deep inside her, focusing on her clit. Soft moans increase with every movement of my tongue.

"Oh, my God, Lance, right there, yes, right there." She sounds breathless. "Don't stop…" She's stubborn and wants to cum but is holding herself back. A slight change of pace is needed and then she loses the fight.

"Please, don't tease me." Her breathing increases. "I-I c-can't…" Her eyes roll back as pleasure threatens to overwhelm her.

"That's one," I move back and mumble words to myself. Moving my fingers gently over her g-spot, I'm granted another moan. I slow my movements, prolonging my own agony while anticipating at least one more plea.

"Lance, please…" Her breathing quickens and I can feel her legs tremble.

"That's two."

With my tongue, I work that perfect spot. I can feel my

cock straining against my jeans but it's her pleasure that matters right now, not mine. Suddenly, she yields, and I'm met with instant success as she cries out, "Yes, that's it. Right there."

As she climaxes, I share the same sense of ecstasy and pride. Not because of my skills in the bedroom or the fact I was able to quickly bring her to orgasm but because it was all about her. Still, holding back on my own release was absolute torture.

Now it's my turn.

Quickly, I remove my pants and pull the T-shirt over my head. I anxiously position myself back in place, between her thighs. Her eyes are only half-open, her body trembling, and she has that far away look of blissful satisfaction.

"Are you okay?"

"That was just..." she takes several deep breaths, "...so good."

"And it only gets better from here beautiful."

"There's more?" Her eyes snap open giving a look of surprise.

"Let's get that dress all the way off." She sits up, allowing me to remove it. Tossing the material over my shoulder, it lands on the floor beside my discarded clothing.

Working my way up her body, I circle my tongue around her belly button and brush my lips from hip to hip. Then, sliding my body against hers, I reach her perfect breast and draw one nipple into my mouth, sucking hard.

My rock-hard cock has found its home. I slide into her, relishing her gasp, and with each slow thrust, I push in a little deeper. We move our bodies in unison, each of us taking and giving what we need.

"Faster, harder." Her plea is almost a whisper. My effort to keep going at a slow pace is thwarted when Kellie grabs my hips and guides me closer toward her.

"Slow down." Sweat forms on my brow. "Too, soon." I can barely spit out the words. I don't want to be like the typical virgin on prom night, but it feels too good, and I'm already close.

I can feel her walls clamp around my cock. Suddenly she slows to a stop, giving me more of a fighting chance to hold out a few more minutes.

The urge to fuck her is too strong. Kellie rocks into me and clenches her muscles around my cock. "Keep that up and I'm going to cum." She clenches her muscles again. "Fuuuckk!"

Lacking finesse, I gyrate my hips in a faster motion, and with one last thrust, my control slips just as the spasms begin to rack her body.

Our lips meet. I drink her in. "I love you." *Shit*. The words escape before I can reign them in. My inability to hold my tongue makes me feel like an ass. Post orgasm was not how I planned to tell Kellie how much she means to me. I've turned what should be a special moment into a cheap after sex clichéd meaningless declaration of love.

Mentally berating myself for screwing this up, my mind is eased when she responds, "I love you too." Her eyes well up with unshed tears. This time she initiates the kiss. I stop overanalyzing it and realize it doesn't matter when we say it, only that we feel it.

My stomach grumbles loudly, interrupting the moment. Kellie laughs while her lips are still touching mine. She rolls me over and straddles my hips. Poking my belly, she says, "You sound like a big old hungry bear."

"I'm starving."

"So I heard."

"Being with you has worked up my appetite." Brushing hair back from her brow, I swear I see a glow of satisfaction on her face. "Are you hungry?"

She nods. "Famished. I want pizza, some chicken wings, and those breadstick things with ranch dressing and maybe chocolate cake." I raise an eyebrow, wondering if she plans to eat all that food. "What? I had a workout too, ya know."

She cracks me up. "Okay, tell you what. How about a quick shower? Then we can order food and watch a movie."

"Sounds perfect to me." She jumps up and races to the bathroom. "First one in picks the movie."

"Cheater." I race after her, not caring one bit if she wins. I'll happily let her choose every movie we watch for the rest of our lives.

Kellie's stretched out on the couch with her feet on my lap while we watch an old cartoon from Rory's library. "I told you I love these movies."

"Yeah, but I was supposed to pick what we were watching, remember?"

"You did pick. We watched that chick flick, Actually Love." I'm hoping she didn't notice I dozed off somewhere in the middle.

"That's not the title. It's Love Actually, but that's not important." She narrows her eyes. "The real problem was when your snoring drowned out the best part."

"Uh, you saw that, huh?" I grimace.

"Well, I heard you first, but you were too cute to wake up." She stands and clears the to-go boxes from the table.

I follow her to the kitchen with our plates and load them into the dishwasher. "I know you said you aren't mad, but I hate what happened at Heath's and how it almost ruined our night."

"It's not your fault. Other than our run in with the wicked witch, tonight has been amazing."

"I couldn't agree more." I glance over my shoulder. "Do you want me to turn this on?" My eyes almost pop out of my head when she bends to place the leftovers into the refrigerator shelf. The tiny shorts she put on after our shower ride up, giving me just a peek at her luscious ass. It's too tempting to resist. I sneak up behind her and quickly pinch her booty.

"Hey." She spins quickly to face me.

"You shouldn't put your butt on display like that if you don't want me to give it some attention." She shoots me a silly grin and I kiss the tip of her nose. "Thank you for not letting Patricia ruin our night."

"You know, when I saw her touch you, I wanted to break her wrist." She flashes a devilish smile. I like this possessive side of my girl.

"That would not have been a good idea in front of a room full of cops."

"Yeah, but it would have felt great to knock her on her ass." She makes a fist and punches into her other hand a few times.

"Alright, Rocky. Your turn to pick the next movie."

She links our fingers and leads us back to the living room. "I think that's a great idea. Lead on, Sir Lancelot."

I roll my eyes, loving the sound of her teasing.

"I'm a little confused. Why do you keep calling her Patricia?"

"When I met her, she insisted I use her full name. It's only recently I learned she's gone back to Trish."

"How recently are you talking?" I sit down on the couch and tug her hand for her to cuddle up in my lap. I don't think I'll ever tire of having her in my arms.

"She came to my house the same night we watched movies with Rory in the fort. I told her I'd file a restraining order for stalking if she showed up uninvited again."

"Well, based on what happened at the bar, I'd say she didn't listen."

"This was the first time I've seen her since that day, and you can be certain, first thing Monday morning, I will be in front of a judge requesting the stay away order."

"Will that work?"

I huff out a breath. "I'd like to say yes, but to be honest, probably not. We make arrests all the time for restraining order violations."

"So why bother if she's most likely going to break the law and show up again?"

"Because it's part of the process. Sometimes we get lucky, and people listen and follow the rules, but in this case, I can see she's out of her mind."

"Why do you think that?"

"She was always intense and impulsive when we dated, but I never saw this conniving side of her until tonight."

"So, what happens now?" She snuggles under my chin and I trace circles on her back with my index finger.

"For now, all I care about is keeping you and Rory safe."

"Do you think she would do something crazy?"

"I think she already has, but I can't prove it."

"Huh?"

"I'll bet it was her that vandalized your car, which means she knows where you live. I'd like for you and Rory to stay with me until she is served the papers."

"I can't just up and move Rory like that. Maybe she can stay with my parents for a while."

"Then you can come stay with me."

"Thanks, Lance, but no way."

"It won't be for long."

"Forget it." She is adamant so I better tread carefully. "I refuse to let Trish run me out of my own home. You installed the cameras and alarm system. That should be enough."

I won't fight her on this right now. If I can't convince her to stay with me, at least I know there is security in place. Plus, now I can tell the deputies who to be on the lookout for.

"We can talk about this later. What movie are you choosing?" Please don't let it be another chick flick.

She starts scanning through the list of available movies streaming on her TV. "Shoot, I can't find it." Using the search option, I watch the letters appear on the screen.

P-U-R-P-L-E U-N-I-C-O-R-N

Kellie bites her top lip to hide her smile.

Without any hesitation, I say, "Best. Code. Word. Ever." I jump up from the couch with her still cradled in my arms and practically run down the hall. As we tumble on top of her bed, our combined laughter lifts me further away from the darkness I never thought I'd escape.

15

KELLIE

My nerves are shot.

We've been parked outside Lance's parent's house for five minutes already and I can't seem to stop my hands from shaking. Meeting his family is a monumental step in our relationship. I'm terrified they will hate me.

"Alright, Rory. Are we ready to do this?" I adjust the rearview mirror to look at my niece still buckled into her car seat.

It's the first break in our schedules in weeks, and while it's been smooth sailing, Rory starting preschool hasn't provided us with any free time. Thankfully, she loves it and has already been on a few playdates with her new friends. It's wonderful to watch her grow and see her personality shine.

Rory thriving was a welcome bright spot after Trish was served her restraining order. I had anticipated the worst, but it went better than expected. Gina was embarrassed and apologetic, but I tried to reassure her that there was nothing she could have done differently. Still, Gina feels a level of responsibility since Trish is a family member of hers.

Afterward, I learned Trish's father forced her into a drug

and alcohol rehabilitation program. No expense was spared, and despite my hatred of her, I wish her the best and hope she emerges a better person than she was before.

Lance has finally returned to patrol, and other than a few moments where he needed to talk out his feelings, everything has been great.

Then why do I feel so anxious? *Oh, yeah. Lance's mom is going to hate me.*

"Addy K, I bored."

"Okay, sweetheart, one more minute, and we can go in."

Pull yourself together, Kellie.

I close my eyes, rest my head on the seat and pray this goes well. No mother likes the woman who replaces her in her son's life. My mom shared her own horror stories about how my Dad's mom hated her when they first met. I anticipate the same reaction from Mrs. Malloy.

A knock on my window pulls me back to the here and now. Lance is staring at me with a confused expression. "Are you okay?"

"No. Your mom isn't going to like me. I just know it."

"Will you get out of the car, please?" He opens my door and I take his offered hand.

"Okay, but don't be mad. I'm just nervous." I blow strands of hair that hang in my face while I struggle with Rory's bag.

"Don't be. My mom and dad are going to love both of you."

"If only life was that easy." I unbuckle Rory from her safety seat and hoist her up on my hip.

"Give Rory to me." He holds out his arms, but she turns away when usually she would jump into them. It seems I'm not the only one who's nervous. Rory has snuggled into my neck and popped her thumb into her mouth. She clings onto her new stuffed rabbit that's been everywhere with us for the last month. Though I'm still unsure where it came from, I can't bear to take it away from her.

"Let me take the bag at least." Lance reaches for the large bag full of toys, books, and other things to occupy Rory when she suddenly lets go of me and dives into his arms. She wraps her little arms around his neck. It was so natural. Their bond warms my heart.

"Are you ready?"

"No," I reply, not meaning to sound as moody as I do.

"Let's do this."

I walk closely behind Lance, then past the white wooden gate into the backyard, which is actually a beautifully kept garden with manicured lawns and vibrantly colored flowers.

"You're here." A striking older lady wearing a large, brimmed hat rushes our way. I can only assume she is Lance's mom.

Lance steps aside. "Mom, this is Kellie, and the little monkey clinging onto me is Rory." She giggles when he tickles her side.

"Hello, Rory."

"Say hello to Mrs. Malloy."

"Oh, there's no need to be so formal. Please call me Tracy." Her welcoming smile eases some of my worries.

"I'm so sorry, she's just a little shy."

"Don't worry. Lance was just like her at that age." She pulls me into a hug. "It's so nice to finally meet you."

"She's terrified you'll be one of those mothers who instantly hates the new girlfriend."

I shoot him a look that says he's a dead man walking. "I did not say that."

"Oh, don't you worry. He's just like his father always sticking his big foot in his bigger mouth." She takes the bag from me. "Here, Lance, do something with that. It should keep you out of trouble." I wanted to laugh but didn't.

I was taken aback by her warm welcome. She liked me, I could tell, and I liked her too. "Come with me and I'll introduce you to Lance's father."

With one introduction out of the way I meet his dad. They look strikingly similar, and for a moment, I'm dazzled. He's just as handsome as Lance. Hair trimmed neatly, with streaks of silver. I imagine this is how Lance will look at his age.

"It's nice to meet you, Sir."

"Lance has told us all about you and Rory."

"You'll have to forgive her. She's having a shy moment but will come out of her shell in a few minutes."

"My son is quite captivated by that little girl."

"I think the feeling is entirely mutual." We both watch as Lance sways side to side, speaking softly in Rory's ear.

"Now, while I don't want to dwell in the past, I need to get this out of the way..."

"Dad, please."

"I want to thank you for helping our son find his smile again."

"Oh, God, Mom, tell him..." Lance groans, sounding like a whining teenager.

"Just let me speak my mind, then we don't have to mention it ever again."

"You saved our son." Mr. Malloy's voice softens. I can only imagine what it was like for him and his wife to be out of the country when Lance called.

"He saved me too, and Rory."

"That's true, but for what it's worth, you will always be welcome in our home."

"I don't know what to say."

"You and Rory are family now."

Tears spring to my eyes. "I'm sorry, I'm not usually so emotional."

"Don't apologize." Tracy hands me a handkerchief from her pocket, and I dab at my eyes. "Most people never find true love, but I have high hopes for you and my son."

"Can we change the subject, please? I feel like I'm stuck in a Hallmark Channel loop."

"If he weren't so much like his father, I'd wonder if we actually brought the right baby home from the hospital." Mrs. Malloy shakes her head then points over to the round table set up with snacks. "I hope you're hungry because Lance has bought far too much food."

"I'm starved." My original fears of them not liking me have all but disappeared.

Rory is still clinging to Lance. She finally lifts her head to glance around.

Lance squats and sets Rory on her feet, turning her so she faces Mr. Malloy. He wraps a protective arm around her and whispers, "You don't have to be afraid. I'm right here."

"I'm shy," she announces.

"You don't have to be shy, Rory," Lance speaks in an encouraging tone. "This is my dad."

"You have a daddy?"

"Yep. Just like Grumpa is Aunt Kellie's dad. This is my dad. Can you say hi?"

She tilts her head, sizing him up, and thinks about it. Finally, she speaks. "Hi."

"Hello, Rory. It is wonderful to meet you." He tickles her belly.

"You're a Grumpa too?" Both Lance and his dad laugh.

Lance's Mom steps in. "His name is David."

"Grumpa David?" she asks.

"Well...If Aunt Kellie agrees…" He looks up to me and I nod my approval. "Grumpa David it is."

Rory reaches for Lance's hand and tugs. "I'm hungry."

"Me too. Let's go eat." He sets Rory up at the table and places a slice of watermelon on her plate.

"Rory already loves him so much." Every time I see them together, my heart skips a beat.

"I don't think she's the only one." Lance's mom wraps her arm around my shoulders and says, "Welcome to the family."

~

"We need to hurry if we're making cupcakes for Lance." I tie Rory's child sized chef's apron around her waist and help her up onto the stepstool.

"I want to do it." She reaches for the eggs.

"Whoa, you'll get to help, but I'll crack these." She crosses her arms over her chest and pouts. When I give her the wooden spoon and mixing bowl, she settles down.

"I'll add the ingredients and you can stir."

"Okay."

"What flavor do you think Lance will like?" I hold up two boxes of cake mix.

"Chocolate."

"Chocolate it is." I pour the powder into the bowl with the wet ingredients.

Rory stirs for a bit, then huffs out a breath. "It's too hard."

"Not everything is easy. You have to keep trying. Hang on." I have her step down and place the bowl on the stool, putting it at her level. "See, much easier."

"Now we need the paper cups." I search through the pantry and find what I need. When I turn back around, Rory is licking the batter off the large wooden spoon. A big dollop of chocolate falls onto the floor. "Just what do you think you are doing, Missy?"

"It smelled sooo good. I wanted a lick." With batter

smeared over her cheeks and those adorable, puppy dog eyes, I can't do anything but laugh.

"Fine, but next time, ask Auntie Kellie, and I can let you have a little taste from a small spoon."

Before I can scoop her up in my arms, she swipes her finger through the batter and pops it into her mouth.

"No more, silly goose. You're going to have a tummy ache. Let's get your face washed and find you some clean clothes."

Just as I pull Rory's new T-shirt over her head, my phone vibrates in my back pocket.

Lance: Hey, babe. I'm going to be late.

Kellie: Really? Again?

I've barely seen Lance over the past three weeks.

I'm beginning to understand what his mom said about being patient, expecting the unexpected, and don't make any plans that can't be changed on a dime.

Lance: Yeah, I'm sorry.

Kellie: Okay. Will you be here for dinner?

Lance: I'll try. I don't know how late I'll be.

Kellie: Just be safe. I love you.

. . .

Lance: I love you too.

Rory and I finish baking the cupcakes. I smear white frosting on the top, then fill a piping bag with royal blue icing.

"I do it." Rory grabs for the pastry bag.

"Wait. Let's do this together." Placing one of the cupcakes in front of her, I show her how to pipe on the letters. "I'll hold the bag and you can help squeeze."

"Okay." We make a game of it by singing the alphabet and stopping when we get to the letter we need to write.

It takes longer and is messier than if I did it myself, but I want Rory to have unforgettable memories like I have with my mom and Leslie. Plus, I know Lance will appreciate it more knowing she and I did this together.

When all is said and done, Rory and I succeed in writing a message to our deputy.

WE LOVE YOU LANCE

Looking at the clock again, I see it's almost 7pm and Lance still isn't here.

"Addy K, I'm hungry. You said Lance was coming?" Her disappointment matches my own. I tried holding off as long as possible for dinner, but Rory needs to eat.

"I know, but he's still at work. How about we eat our dinner and maybe he will be here for dessert?"

"Yes. My tummy is rumbly."

"You go sit down and I'll get your plate." She rushes to the table and sits in her booster seat. "Do you want apple juice or milk?"

"Apple." I hand her the cup of juice and place a yellow happy face plate with chicken nuggets in front of her.

My stomach growls when I smell the pork loin and roasted garlic potatoes. I dish myself a plate and sit across from her.

Rory shares stories about her friends from school while we eat. My hope for Lance to be here by dessert is crushed. I don't want to call him if he's busy, but I'm also beginning to worry.

Finally, my phone rings just as I finish reading Rory's bedtime story.

"Hang on, Lance is calling us."

"Hello."

"I have bad news." The faint sounds of police sirens are in the background.

"What? Are you okay?" My pulse quickens. Is he hurt? Has he been shot?

"No, I'm fine. Shit. Sorry, I didn't mean to frighten you."

"Don't scare me like that."

"I'm sorry, I need to remember how I say things. I'm not used to having to let someone know I'm working late."

"Yeah, well, I'm new to being the girlfriend of a cop, and you scared the crap out of me." I close my eyes and will my heart rate to slow down. "Now, what's the bad news?"

"Don't hate me, but there's no way I'll make it for dinner."

"I figured as much. We got hungry, so we ate already. I put a plate of food in the fridge if you come by later." I try to mask my frustration. It's not his fault. "I was just putting Rory to bed."

"Can I tell her good night?"

"Sure, hang on." I put him on speaker. "It's Lance."

"Hi, Lance. You missed our surprise."

"I'm so sorry. I'll be there tomorrow, and you can give it to me then."

"It's cupcakes with your name."

I roll my eyes. "It's not a surprise if you tell him."

"Darn it. I love cupcakes. Will you save me one?"

"Yes."

"Thanks, kiddo. You better get some sleep so you're ready for the park tomorrow."

"Okay." She snuggles under the covers. "Night night, Lance."

"Sweet dreams."

I switch the speaker off, tuck the stuffed bunny under her covers, kiss the top of her head and walk to the living room.

"So, this is what life is like in a law enforcement family."

"Unfortunately, yeah. And, this is just the beginning."

"Are you sure you'll be able to make it for our picnic?"

"I wouldn't miss it for the world."

I hear the squelch over his radio, and the dispatcher calls out, "Dispatch to squad 1745; what's your location?"

"I have to go. I love you."

"I love you too." He hung up so fast I'm not sure he heard me.

After covering the cupcakes and putting away the left-overs, I decided to call it a night. A cup of hot tea and a book will have to be my companions of choice tonight.

Picking up my e-reader from my side table, I climb under the covers and choose a new romance about wolf shifters. Just as I get to the part where the wolf pack's alpha is about to make his move on the heroine, my phone lights up.

Lance: Are you still awake?

Kellie: Yes.

. . .

Lance: I'm parked outside your house. Can I come in?

Kellie: Of course.

Although I gave him a key, he won't use it unless I know he's coming over. I open the door and meet him on the front porch. Wiping his boots on the mat, he steps inside and kisses my cheek. Tucked under his arm, he has a cardboard box.

"Here, can you take this?" He hands me the box and sits on the couch. It's lighter than I expected. He removes his duty belt and unlaces his boots.

"What's in here?" I place the box on the coffee table and hear the tiny meow. Lifting the flaps carefully, a small orange and white striped cat pokes its head up through the opening.

"I found her on my last call." He finishes taking his boots off and places them under the table. "A truck slid off the road on a steep curve. While I was waiting for the tow truck, I saw this box in a ditch and checked it out."

Lifting the cat from the box carefully, I tuck her under my chin, holding her close. "Poor baby. And she was inside?"

"Some asshole taped it closed. I don't think she was there very long. I'll take her to animal control tomorrow." Lance yawns and I notice the dark circles under his eyes. The overtime is catching up to him.

"She must be starving. Why don't you get changed and I'll see what I can find for her to eat?"

Searching the fridge, I find deli turkey and break off a few small pieces. The cat sniffs a few times, then chews quickly. She licks at my fingers and I give her a bit more. "You have to slow down, sweetie, or you'll get sick. Let's get you some water."

I decide to put the cat in my guest bathroom for the night. Filling a bowl with water, I place it in front of the bathmat. She laps at the liquid then curls into a ball, barely able to keep her eyes open. I scratch between her ears a few times and her purring gets louder. "You're safe now. Get some rest, little one."

Closing the door behind me, I walk past my bedroom door and freeze when I see Lance undressing. My eyes pop open at the sight of my sexy officer. He unbuttons his uniform shirt revealing his ballistic vest. It's every woman's fantasy and he's mine. Slipping off his shirt, I see his muscles flex and lean on the wall for support.

"Are you enjoying the show?"

Busted.

"What's not to like. It's my very own Chippendale's show." I sit on the end of the bed and watch as he removes the rest of his clothes.

"I'll gladly strip for you, anytime you like." His cocky grin shows off his dimples.

With just his boxer briefs on, I take a minute to admire his body. I unabashedly look him up and down, memorizing every inch of the man I love.

"Why don't you go shower and I'll put your uniform in the laundry room?" I take the clothes from him and drape them over my arm.

He wraps me up in his arms and kisses me tenderly.

"Only if you promise to join me."

"I think I can arrange that."

I hang his uniform on the clothes rack and run my finger over the star on his shoulder patch. There is still a lot to consider about how his job will affect our lives. Tonight was just a taste of the late hours and sudden changes in his schedule. What I do know is I love Lance and that means learning to make it work.

Walking back into my bedroom, I expect to hear the shower, but instead, I see Lance passed out cold on the bed. I guess there won't be any sexy time tonight.

I crawl in beside him and pull blankets over us. He pulls me close and I can't help but feel safe in his arms. With my head on his chest, I allow the beating of his heart to lull me to sleep.

~

We arrive at the park around noon. The weather is warm, with just a cool breeze. It's the perfect day for a picnic. For the first time, I feel like we are a family, and although we still have a lot to talk about, I wonder if this could be what our future might look like.

"How about over there?" Lance points to a shady spot under a tree.

"That works." It's close to the swings and sandbox Rory loves to dig in.

"I wanna play." Rory jumps up and down impatiently. "Lance, will you take me?"

"Why don't we eat lunch first?" I answer before he can agree since he rarely tells her no.

"How about you help me spread out the blanket?" Rory takes a corner from Lance and does her best to make it straight. "Good job." He praises her effort.

"Let's see what we have for lunch." I open the plastic cooler and remove sandwiches and a bowl of fruit. Rory sits in Lance's lap and shares a bag of chips. They take turns feeding each other. When she intentionally misses his mouth, her giggles are contagious. The love that exists between them is evident. He's the only father figure she's ever known. I couldn't ask for anyone better to fill that missing piece in her life.

"Rory, come over here." She sits next to me and digs into her lunch.

"Who made these delicious sandwiches?" Lance asks, taking another bite.

"I did. And I got to cut the melon too."

"No wonder it's so tasty." He pops a cube of cantaloupe into his mouth, making yummy noises as he chews.

In between bites, Rory tells stories about what she did at school that week.

"What was your favorite part?" I ask while cleaning up our lunch wrappers.

"When we fingerpainted our names. I did really good. R O R Y spells Rory." She says the letters slowly but with complete confidence.

"I'm so proud of you. You must be the best speller in the school." Lance is overreaching here, but I love how he encourages her.

"Addy K, can I go to the slide?"

"Yeah, hang on." I stand up, intending to go with her.

"Look, there's my friend Carl." She points to a small boy with glasses. Mud is smeared across his knees. I recognize him from her preschool. "Can I go play with him?"

"Let's go." When I reach for her hand, she doesn't take it. "What's wrong?"

"I do it myself." The school has been incredible but has given her a level of independence I'm not sure I'm ready for.

"No, I need to stay with you." She'll be four soon, but it seems too young to allow her to play without me standing close by. I look around the play structure and see most of the parents sitting around the area, allowing their kids to play independently. Maybe I'm doing this wrong, and I've become one of those helicopter parents. "Do you think I'm overreacting?"

"You can never be too careful, but I think she'll be fine.

We can see her from here. Why not let her play with the kids?" Lance has stretched out on the blanket, leaning against the tree.

I hesitate but decide to give in. "Fine but stay where I can see you. Do not leave the playground. Understand?"

Rory nods and takes off at a full sprint. She says something to her friend, and they hold hands while walking to the mini log cabin.

I remain standing and watch her for a few minutes. "My little girl isn't such a baby anymore."

"See, she's fine. Now relax." Lance reaches up to me and I take his hand.

I position myself between his splayed legs and lean back against his chest.

A child screams, causing me to jump. Instantly my eyes search out Rory.

"I'm watching her. Look, she's having fun," Lance reassures me. He pulls his phone from his pocket and takes a picture of her playing with the other kids, flipping it around for me to see. "Look how happy she is." When I see her climbing the stairs to the slide with a wide grin, I sink back against him. "You can't hover over her forever."

"I know, but it's easier said than done." Using my fingernail, I absently trace hearts on Lance's open palm. "You know I have to keep that cat now that Rory has named her."

"Is that such a bad thing? Think of the responsibilities you can teach her about caring for an animal."

"I guess a cat is better than the puppy she's been begging for."

"Exactly, and Tiger needs someone to love on her. She's had a hard start in life, just like Rory. Maybe they were meant to be friends."

"Cheater. You sure know how to tug at my heartstrings with that comparison."

When Rory asked me this morning if we could keep it, I hesitated and told her I would decide later, but in my heart, I knew she would stay. I can't imagine bringing her to animal control and risking them euthanizing her.

Trying to relax, I take a deep breath and fill my lungs with the scent of fresh cut grass. The sound of children laughing and having fun are what summer days are made for. Perhaps Lance is right, and I need to allow Rory more breathing space.

"Addy K, watch me!" Rory stands at the top of the slide and calls out to me.

"I see you!" I wave and watch her slip down with her hands in the air. I'm still not entirely comfortable with her playing away from me, even if it is a short distance, but I must learn to give her more freedom. I watch with pride as her feet hit the sand and she rushes back toward the log cabin.

Stepping out from behind one of the large redwood trees surrounding the park, Trish frowns in the direction of Lance and Kellie.

After following them for weeks, today provides the perfect opportunity to drive a wedge between the lovebirds. She knows once Kellie is out of the picture, Lance will return to her, and things will go back to how they are meant to be.

Trish waves to Rory, flashing a big, warm smile. She motions for her to come closer.

"Hello again, Rory. Do you remember me?"

Rory nods. "You gave me my bunny."

"That's right, I did," she replies in a cutesy voice. "Where is he?"

"Addy K said he had to stay at home."

"Aw, that's a shame. I bet you miss him?"

"Yeah."

"Guess what? I found a momma bunny and her babies. Would you like to see them?"

"Where are they?"

"Come with me and I'll show you." Trish holds her hand out, but Rory is hesitant.

"Addy K says I can't leave."

"It will be okay. Lance and Addy K are my friends. They told me to show you the bunnies while they finished talking."

Rory looks to where Lance and Kellie are sitting under the tree then back to Trish.

"Come on, we'll be super quick." Rory takes Trish's hand and follows her deeper into the grove of trees. "We have to be very quiet. The babies might be sleeping."

A young couple walks past where Lance and I are sitting. I see the man has a tiny baby strapped to his chest. The empty ache in my heart I've felt lately when seeing pregnant women and babies returns. It's a subject I've meant to talk with Lance about, but the timing has never seemed right.

"Lance? There's something important I need to ask you." I sit up and spin around to face him.

"Okay. This sounds serious. What's on your mind?" He sits up a little straighter.

"This may be too soon to talk about." I chew on my lip and my fingers twist in my lap. "Here's the thing. I know I have Rory already and you're great with her. But I was wondering what you think about having kids of your own."

"Is that what has you worried? Come here." I sit in his lap. He cups my cheeks and kisses me softly. Against my lips, he whispers, "Kel, I want to spend the rest of my life with you.

And Rory. I want children, and if we are blessed to have more, that is wonderful. If Rory is the only child we have, then I'm okay with that too."

"I want a baby, but I feel guilty. It would split my time and doesn't seem fair to Rory."

"Are you kidding? Rory would make a great big sister."

"I think you're right."

"So, does this mean you want to marry me?" He takes my hand in his and I tense up.

"Uh… I mean, wait…" Shit, I didn't mean for our conversation to go this direction. Is he actually proposing or just asking a general question?

The familiar bells of an ice cream cart ring, giving me an excuse to change the subject.

"I want ice cream." I jump out of his arms, grateful for the distraction.

An older man pushing an ice cream cart stops next to the playground and rings his bell again. The kids abandon what they are doing and scatter, I assume, to ask their parents for money.

"Smart man. He will sell out in no time." Lance stands beside me with his hands on my shoulders.

"Where's Rory?" I scan the group of children now surrounding the cart, waiting to order.

"She was just here. I'm sure she's hiding in the cabin. I'll go check." Lance jogs to the other side just out of sight.

"Rory!" I call out, trying not to panic. "Rory! Where are you!"

Lance runs back to me, the color gone from his face. "S-she's…" He stumbles over his words. "S-She's gone."

"Maybe she went to the bathroom." I sprint to the nearby building checking every stall, but it's empty. When I return, Lance is speaking calmly with Carl and his mom.

"I'm sorry, I haven't seen her since Carl came over to eat

his lunch." As my tears fall, she lifts her son protectively into her arms. "Let me take him to his father and I can help you search for her."

"Rory!" I cup my hands around my mouth and shout again.

"I'm calling dispatch. You keep asking around if anyone has seen anything." Lance steps away from the playground and the chaos to make his call.

I race from parent to parent, asking if they have seen my little girl, giving her description and the clothes she has on. "Have you seen my little girl? She was just here, pink shirt with pigtails. Her name's Rory." I hold my breath, hoping I'll get a tiny piece of information that will lead me to my niece.

"I saw her playing earlier. I'm sorry, I didn't notice anything out of the ordinary." The young mother cradles her baby close and my body trembles as I rush to the next person.

"Ma'am, let us help you. What's her name?" A crowd has gathered around me.

"Her name is Rory. Please help me find her."

Several adults are now searching the surrounding area, calling out her name.

The world seems to spin around me, and my heart feels like it's banging against my rib cage. White spots dance before my eyes.

"Where are you, baby?" My heart is pounding, ready to burst out from my chest. "Rory!" I shout again.

"The deputies are on their way to help us search. Has anyone seen her?"

"NO!" I yell at him. "Why the fuck are you so calm?"

"Because I have a job to do right now and losing control won't help us find her any faster."

"This isn't just any job, Lance. And if you were doing your

job, she wouldn't be missing." I'm close to losing my shit, but I know he's right. I must keep it together for Rory's sake.

"We'll find her. I promise." Lance tries to pull me toward him, but I push him away. It only serves to light the fire within me, and finally, I lose what's left of my composure.

"This is your fault," I scream accusingly. "I didn't want to let her play by herself and you said she'd be fine." I run to the other side of the play structure with Lance close behind. "You're a cop. You need to find her now!" I see a chink in his armor, and tears fill his eyes right before he runs to the other side of the park shouting for my baby.

My eyes dart about in the hope I'll see her, that wherever she's hiding, she'll know I'm going crazy. "RORY," I cry. "Please come out now, Addy K is scared."

My throat hurts from screaming, but I refuse to stop until I find her.

"My baby," I whisper, feeling like every ounce of energy has been stolen from me. Falling to my knees, I hold my hands over my heart and pray. *Please, God, don't take her from me. I'll do anything, just help me find her.*

"Kellie, let me..." Lance is standing in front of me and tries to help me to my feet, but I shrug him off.

I won't give up. I can't. Taking another deep breath, I scream at the top of my lungs. "RORY!"

To be continued.

ALSO BY THE AUTHOR

The Weight of the Badge - Book Three

Out of the Blue

https://geni.us/oJzKlb

For *Kellie, life was almost perfect.*

She'd found the man of her dreams in Lance, and finally consigned their initial problems to the past.

But then, facing *what can only be described as every parent's worst nightmare, her world is torn apart, and she is forced to defend her family from the person lurking in the shadows.*

Refusing to be terrorized, Kellie must fight for those she loves the most, but at what cost?

For Lance, after the loss of his best friend, he'd found a reason to live again, and with a ready-made family in Kellie and Rory, everything he'd ever wished for seemed to be within his grasp.

But someone hides in plain sight, desperate to stand in the way of his happiness.

To secure a future with the woman he loves, and the little girl he has come to see as his own, Lance must prove he is capable of protecting them all.

For the Love of Us;

Fighting to Keep Our Love Alive

geni.us/ftlouFB

What happens when the kids leave for college, and you remember you're not just mom, but a woman too?

Simply going through the motions, on autopilot day after day, weighed heavily on me.

The one thing which bonded my husband and me, before the kids came along, was slowly cast aside as their needs grew more demanding.

Intimacy became an act; a performance, without the desire, passion, and lust we once shared.

My need to feel desired and wanted by my husband ate at me and I was determined to make him see the woman he married.

I wasn't going to give up and hatched a plan, one which would hopefully forge a new beginning for us.

Fighting to keep our love alive was a risk, but, for us, I was prepared to do anything.

ACKNOWLEDGMENTS

To my husband and sons, thank you for always believing in me. Life isn't always easy, but we make it work. I love you more.

Gloria Nuckols and Zane Michaelson, thank you for your continued support and friendship.

To all the authors, PA's, readers, and friends who have supported me on this journey thank you.

To my editor, Mina, thank you for your guidance and for not allowing me to settle for anything less than my best.

THANK YOU~Kaylee Rose xoxo

ABOUT THE AUTHOR

Kaylee Rose is a wife, mother, sports fan, and contemporary romance author looking to stretch her creative muscles and explore other genres as well.

Born and raised in a small beach town just outside San Francisco, California, Kaylee is the mother of four sons. Inspired by her husband's career in law enforcement, and her passion for the written word, Kaylee began to pen her novels as an escape from the rigors of everyday life.

Kaylee's series The Weight of the Badge was written after attending law enforcement classes with her husband. The seminars focused on the stress a first responder faces daily, how it affects their lives both on and off the job, and the continually growing number of law enforcement suicides. With her books and her experience married to a law enforcement officer, Kaylee found herself armed with the perfect platform to use her voice and subtly spread the statistics others may not know. Kaylee Rose is passionate about sharing sexy stories with an important message mixed in.

Kaylee's husband is her biggest supporter, believing in her even when she can not, and writing love stories comes naturally to her after falling in love with him at first sight.

Her happy place is Disneyland with her family or going on a road trip, or camping with her hubby.

For more information or just to touch base with Kaylee, you will find her at:

Official Website: https://authorkayleerose.com

Facebook Author Page https://tinyurl.com/yc5e7gvb

Newsletter: https://tinyurl.com/yaoar9e2

Instagram: https://instagram.com/authorkayleerose

Twitter: https://twitter.com/AuthorKayleeYouTube

YouTube Channel: https://tinyurl.com/yaggl8z7

RESOURCES

Resources for officers and their family members who may be struggling.

CopLine offers a confidential 24-hour hotline answered by retired law enforcement officers who have gone through a strenuous vetting and training process to become an active listener.

Copline peer listeners provide assistance with the successful management of various psychosocial stressors that impact a significant number of law enforcement officers and their families.
https://www.copline.org
Hotline: 1-800-COPLINE (267-5463)

Safe Call Now is a confidential, comprehensive, 24-hour crisis referral service for all public safety employees, all emergency services personnel, and their family members nationwide.
SAFE CALL NOW: 1-206-459-3020

NATIONAL SUICIDE PREVENTION LIFELINE
1-800-273-TALK (8255)

Global Suicide Hotline Resources
WhatsApp https://tinyurl.com/yb3jn6jf

Under the Shield
https://undertheshield.com/
https://www.facebook.com/undertheshield14/
(855) 889-2348

Made in the USA
Monee, IL
28 June 2022